I0589898

THE THIEF OF HEARTS

BY

ELIZABETH ELLEN CARTER

with bonus story
THREE SHIPS

CONTENTS

ACKNOWLEDGEMENTS

I would like to thank two amazing people for all their wonderful help and support –
Susanne Bellamy for her insightful observations and my darling husband Duncan Carling-Rodgers for his passion for accuracy and demand for logic, even in the most illogical situations.

THE THIEF OF HEARTS

"Illusion is the first of all pleasures."

– Voltaire

CHAPTER ONE

London
December, 1890

C aroline Addison had been kissed under the mistletoe once before and hadn't much cared for it. On second thoughts, she reflected, perhaps *disappointed* was a better description.

She brushed a hand down her velvet dress – very nearly the colour of the glossy green leaves of the kissing bough suspended over the centre of the drawing room.

Mind you, she wasn't sure what she had been expecting when Bertie kissed her last Christmas, but it was wet, soft, and mushy – much like the weather outside – and certainly not the 'endless bliss' that John Keats waxed so poetic about.

Now Bertie was heading towards her with a look that suggested he hoped the act would be repeated.

Caro readied a polite smile and an excuse.

Albert Stringer – Bertie to his friends – was not a bad soul. He was lanky-framed with a flop of light brown hair falling over his brow and an uneven smile that, on first appearances, made him look ungainly.

But Caro liked him a lot. Truly, she did. But he was so much like her older brother Edward, it had come as a shock when Bertie kissed her. And in the twelve months since, Bertie had spent almost as much time here as he did in his own home. It could only mean one thing – he was contemplating a proposal of marriage.

She sorely wished he wouldn't.

"I think I shall sit the next dance out," she said aloud.

Seated alongside, Caro's best friend Margaret giggled. "It serves you right. I told you not to wear those new shoes to the performance tonight. They needed to be stretched in."

True, Caro conceded silently. The shoes *had* pinched her feet for the entire magic show tonight at the Palladian, but she needed an excuse now, so any port in a storm.

Bertie bowed to them needlessly, a tease born of easy familiarity.

"Ladies, could I entreat one of you to dance?"

Caro was forced to concede to herself that Bertie looked dapper in his evening dress and she was sorry to disappoint him because he was really quite a good dancer. However, while he was in this mood, it was best not to encourage him.

She shifted in her chair to look at Margaret who reminded her of one of those dainty Dresden dolls, yellow hair like spun silk, rosy pink cheeks on porcelain skin and eyes as blue as the summer day. They were the same colour as the dress she wore. If anyone could inspire a man to poetry after just one kiss, it would more likely be her.

The smile she gave was all it took for Bertie's eyes to slide right past Caro's own and bask in the warmth of Margaret's.

"I'd be delighted," she told him, "as long as I can choose the music."

Margaret rose and accepted Bertie's arm. Caro watched them cross the room to where Edward and his fiancée Gwen were at the polyphon, examining the selection of large brass discs.

The upright German music box was her mother's pride and joy. Her father, being the lawyer he was, had nearly fainted at the cost, but had come around when he discovered there were discs that played *his* favourite tunes as well. Now the device had become quite the sensation in their social circle.

Edward wound up the clockwork mechanism and secured a musical disc into its spindle. When he released the lever, the disc began rotating slowly like a hypnotic clock face. The opening notes of The Blue Danube tinkled out of the sound box and the four young people waltzed around the centre of the room.

Caro smiled at them as she made her way to the fireplace, exaggerating a slight limp as she went for the benefit of her excuse.

By the fire, a card table covered in green baize had been set up and her parents played cribbage with Sir Hubert Gilfroy and Lady Constance, and Bertie's parents, Mr and Mrs Stringer.

Seated in a wingback chair located on the other side of the fireplace was Caro's widower uncle Walter, his eyes closed and legs stretched out, blue smoke from his pipe drawn towards the fire. Despite being five years older than her father, Uncle Walter was a man still full of vim and vigour.

Beside him, discarded by the leg of the chair, was today's copy of The Argus. Caro quietly picked it up and looked at the front page story.

THE PHANTOM STRIKES AGAIN!

The main headline was stretched across the width of the page and the one underneath was not much smaller.

The Yard flummoxed by daring diamond thief!

Caro glanced sympathetically at her uncle and silently read on.

Another daring escapade by The Phantom last night and another haul of jewellery – this time belonging to Lady Havershire – now bringing this audacious criminal nearly £20,000 pounds of expensive jewellery in the past three months.

His nocturnal escapades remain untroubled by Scotland Yard who as yet have no clue to the thief's identity, nor it would seem, any plan for his capture.

Chief Inspector Walter Addison refused to speculate on—

"Now Caro, you know better than to believe everything you read in the press."

She started and dropped the paper. Her uncle smiled, his eyes still closed. He removed the pipe from his lips.

"How did you know I was—"

"I overheard you beg off a dance with Albert; I smelled your perfume beside me... and, like all young people, you're burning with curiosity about The Phantom."

His eyes opened as Caro lowered herself into the matching wingback chair opposite her uncle.

"It's the science of deduction," he said with a merry twinkle of mischief in his eyes.

Caro laughed. "Are you taking lessons from Mr Conan-Doyle's detective?"

Uncle Walter took a ruminating puff from his pipe before answering.

"I should be – according to the papers at any rate. No, I read Sherlock Holmes for pleasure."

"I'd have thought you would have enough of crime without taking it home with you."

"It relaxes me."

Caro leaned down to pick up the paper again and skim the article once more. The sensationalist report elicited only four main facts: Lady Havershire's jewels were taken from her locked safe, there was no sign of forced entry – either into the house or the safe, there had been no strangers to the house, and the staff were all above reproach.

"Are you sure the servants aren't lying?" Caro asked. Seeing she had her uncle's attention she leaned in further.

"Or perhaps the good Lady herself was," she whispered, "a... *moral hazard*."

"Then who do you cite in your case for the prosecution?" prompted Sir Hubert from the card table.

Caro felt herself growing red and it wasn't just from the heat of the fire.

She turned, now conscious of the card players over her shoulder who had stopped to listen in. She had just started her second year studying law at St Anne's College, Oxford, and, of all her peers, was considered the most able debater of her year.

She took a deep breath to answer. "None, actually. It's just the facts of the case don't make sense. One of them has to be wrong – either there is physical evidence which has been overlooked – which I know your men are too fastidious to miss," she added to Uncle Walter, "– or the staff are lying, or Lady Havershire is.

"So, in the absence of signs of the safe being tampered with and no one but the mistress of the house being aware of the combination, then Occam's Razor suggests the prime suspect must be Lady Havershire herself."

She looked at her audience. Sir Hubert frowned and Constance, his pretty wife who was older than Caro by only a couple of years, looked bewildered. Bertie's parents, a couple aged in their late sixties, were more difficult to read. She turned to her parents. Her mother wore her disapproval plainly, but her father, she judged, carried a look of endorsement in his eyes.

Everyone always told her she took more after her father than her mother in temperament as well as looks – Caro and Edward carried their father's light brown hair colouring and a particular shape of hazel eyes which was long an Addison trait – even her uncle had it.

Caro turned to him. His pipe was between his lips once more.

Uncle Walter seemed every one of his fifty-five years at this moment – deep lines around his mouth, jowls at his cheeks that disappeared when he grinned – which was often. Caro had been told his nickname at Scotland Yard was Bulldog and she had to confess the resemblance was really quite remarkable.

"More's the pity they won't admit women as barristers," he said. "You'd make a fine prosecutor. But no, I don't believe Lady Havershire is involved."

"How so?"

Walter removed the pipe from his lips once more and tapped the ashy remains of his tobacco into the fire.

"*Instinct* – thirty-five years of it from being a Peeler on the streets to a Chief Inspector at Scotland Yard," he said.

Caro shook her head at that wholly insubstantial reasoning. "There has to be more than simple instinct. What about evidence? What about clues?"

Walter did not answer. He reached into his waist coat pocket and pulled out a supple brown leather pouch to silently refill his pipe. Caro caught her mother's sharp grey eyes.

"*Caroline.*"

She inwardly cringed at the use of her full name.

Her mother regarded her sternly, her playing cards still draped over her fingers like an open fan. "Please ask the servants if supper is ready."

Caro was well aware her mother believed she was wasting her father's time and money studying for a law degree she would never be allowed to use. It was an old argument and one her mother knew was of no use to revive since Caro had gained her father's backing to work in his office as an article clerk, saying it was a more profitable use of her time and education than just sitting at home waiting for a husband to come along.

Excusing herself, Caro crossed from the drawing room through the townhouse foyer towards the dining room, where she heard the clatter of dishes and the delicious smell of something savoury being brought from the kitchen.

Supper was obviously about to be served so she turned to go back to the drawing room when there was sharp tap at the front door. Caro went over and opened it before the footman arrived.

Two men in dark blue cloaks filled the door way, their shoulders hunched against the cold.

"Evening Miss, Sergeants Smith and Parkes of Scotland Yard," announced the older one. He was ruddy faced, and his straight bushy black eyebrows looked like soot smudges. The younger man didn't make much of an impression given most of his face was swathed in a maroon scarf. "Sorry to disturb you but we understand Inspector Addison is here."

Caro directed them to the study and sent the late-arriving footman to fetch her uncle. She met him at the door, told him his sergeants awaited, and went back to the drawing room to announce supper was ready. However, she made sure she was the last to leave the drawing room, as much to avoid being escorted by Bertie as it was to linger by the study door she had purposely left ajar.

"We've tracked down a possible lead, sir," said Smith. "Our man from the theatre reported back earlier this evening and—"

The door closed fully and Caro heard no more.

CHAPTER TWO

H uge puffs of steam billowed hot and clammy onto the platform as the train pulled into the station. A porter opened the carriage door. Caro stood, as did Margaret and Gwen, and they waited for Bertie and Edward to alight.

Bertie took a hold of Caro's hand and gave it a squeeze as he did so. The five friends huddled in the centre of the platform; an island standing firm against the tide of travellers sweeping past. The smell of damp clothing from embarking passengers competed with the acrid smell of burning coal from the locomotive. Caro wrinkled her nose.

"Where to, ladies?" asked Edward.

"The Barrington Arcade is the closest." Gwen answered for all of them. "The rain is absolutely rotten and I'm positive it got worse when we pulled into the station."

As they buttoned up coats and secured scarves around their necks, the group debated for a few moments whether or not to take one of the horse-drawn trams before deciding to brave the two block dash.

They pressed through crowded streets towards the sound of a brass band's music that blared through the driving rain. The music grew louder and the crowd thicker as they approached the Barrington Arcade. Artificial light drew them like a beacon towards the three storey high building with its arched skylight roof and beautiful scrolling stone pediment.

Standing under a shop awning, half a dozen men and women seemed to blend into the gloom, their uniforms of black relieved only by the slash of red satin on their caps and the polished brass of a tuba and trumpets. A flash of a silver hand bell reflected the gaslight and a small sign proclaimed the musicians to be a Salvation Army band.

Caro was pleased to escape the rain, but made sure to open her purse and drop some coins into the collection cauldron in passing as the choir and band started on a new carol. The tune followed them into the arcade.

> *God rest you merry, gentlemen*
> *Let nothing you dismay*
> *For Jesus Christ, our Saviour*
> *Was born upon this day,*
> *To save us all from Satan's power*
> *When we were gone astray.*
> *O tidings of comfort and joy...*

Inside, the lights of the Barrington Arcade banished the darkness. It glowed golden with Christmas cheer. Well-lit shops displayed their festive wares in the bay windows. Between each shop was a green potted conifer – only three feet in height – decorated as a miniature Christmas tree.

In the gallery above, swags of artificial winter greenery were bedecked with gold baubles and red satin ribbons, each length draped in festoons across one side of the void and back, from one end of the Arcade to the other.

Edward tapped Caro on the shoulder.

"You buy the gift for mother from the both of us and I'll buy the one for father. Agreed?"

She grinned. "Can I buy my gift from you? It means it will be something I can actually wear this year."

"I think that's a splendid idea, Caro," Gwen said, squeezing Edward's arm affectionately. "I think I shall do the same."

The group laughed, including Edward.

They agreed to meet up again at the Tudor Inn cake emporium for afternoon tea then the party split up. Edward and Bertie disappeared into the crowd of shoppers.

"Wouldn't it be fun if we could make all these crowds disappear like the magician did to his assistant in the show last night?" said Margaret, sidestepping a reluctant child being dragged along by his fraught mother. "I thought the magician was ever so clever – and handsome too."

"I wonder how he did it?" mused Gwen.

"How did he become handsome?" Caro chimed in. "I think that's a natural gift."

Her friends laughed.

"No, I mean make the girl materialise out of nowhere," said Gwen.

"Don't forget the dove." Margaret rejoined.

"Oh yes, the dove, and the scarves too."

Caro listened to the back and forth of the conversation for a moment.

"It has to be a trick," she said.

"Of course it's a trick!" said Gwen, sweeping raindrops off her teal green coat.

"I think we're all agreed there's nothing supernatural about it," said Caro, "but aren't you just a little bit curious to know *how* 'The Dark Duke' does it?"

"Well, not *me*," Margaret answered firmly, holding her purple reticule close to her side. "It would just ruin the whole thing. I think there is something just a little bit special about being amazed and simply going along with the wonder of the unexpected. You know, when your heart pounds and you grow breathless with anticipation… well, it's a little like falling in love really."

Caro was not convinced. "I think I'd want to know how it was done."

Gwen and Margaret both groaned.

"You need to let go. Stop trying to control everything, Caro," Gwen advised. "Otherwise you'll miss the man who'll sweep you off your feet."

Avoid him, more like, Caro thought. But she said nothing, pleased her friends' attention now turned to shopping. They entered each shop as they made their way along the arcade, discussing the suitability of this object or that as a gift for family, friends or a favourite household member of staff.

Soon, Caro came to a stop three-quarters of the way down, suddenly captivated by a jewellery store window display.

"The perfect thing for Mother!"

She hurried in with the other girls following, the bell jingling to announce the trio's arrival. The jewellery box that caught her eye in the window was beautifully made – figured elm with an ebonised border, offset with mother of pearl stylised foliage and chrysanthemums. It would have been far too expensive if not for Edward's financial contribution added to her own savings from her clerk's wages over the past six months.

All three looked further at the display of exquisite jewellery. Margaret selected a small gold posy ring in blue enamel, set with seed pearls, for *her* mother and Gwen examined a pretty pair of gold filigree earrings as her self-selected gift from Edward.

Something more caught Caro's eye.

Sitting high on top of the glass fronted cabinet behind the jeweller, mounted on a stand backed with black velvet, was the most magnificent diamond brooch she had ever seen. It was in the shape of a butterfly and every facet of it was covered in diamonds. Dangling from its abdomen was a large pear-shaped diamond pendant.

The jeweller caught the direction of her gaze and beamed.

"It's a work of art, is it not?"

"It's breathtaking!"

"Would you like a closer look?"

"May we?" three voices chorused.

The old man's smile broadened even more if possible.

"It is a delight to see three fine young ladies appreciating quality like this," he said and nodded to his younger assistant who used a wooden stepper to climb up. The young man stretched on tip-toes to bring down the display, and, with a reverence to match the jewel's importance and value, he gently placed it on the counter.

"I'm afraid I can't let you try the piece on but you may touch," the jeweller told them.

Gwen brushed her fingers over the fine metal mounts. The jeweller proudly informed them they were platinum and, although silver in colour, far more expensive than silver and indicative of the money lavished on the jewels and their setting.

"Did *you* make it?" Gwen asked.

The jeweller shook his head. "I would like to take credit for this but alas, that would be a lie. The butterfly portion was made in the 18th century by a court jeweller in France. It came to England with the émigrés. And about fifty years ago, the owner had the diamond drop put on it."

"I daren't ask how much," Margaret breathed. She seemed afraid to even touch it.

Caro reached forward and felt the weight of the pendulous diamond on her fingertips.

"I'm afraid this is worth much more than we could ever afford even if we all pooled our Christmas money together for years!"

The jeweller's assistant returned the sparkling butterfly to its high perch.

"A very tempting target for The Phantom," Caro observed.

"No fear there, Miss," said the young assistant, who, if she was not mistaken was attempting a flirtation with her. "We have a huge safe out the back with a combination *and* a key."

The young man hiked a thumb over his shoulder and grinned. "And the only way in is through this door – steel reinforced and locked every night, just like the front door is when we leave. *And* there's a beadle what does the rounds."

Behind Caro, the door opened and the merry little bell rang once again.

"I thought we might find you all in here!"

The three young women turned to greet Edward and Bertie.

"Are you ladies going to linger in here all afternoon? I'm quite famished," said Edward. Gwen excused herself to join her fiancé and to discreetly direct him to the display of earrings in the window.

"At least Gwen will get exactly what she wants for Christmas," Caro whispered. Margaret giggled.

Bertie cast his eye across a display of rings and then looked up at Caro.

"Have you seen anything here you like?"

"Caro showed a partiality to that one there," said Margaret, pointing to a tray of rings which contained a pretty band of small rubies and diamonds she had admired.

Caro felt her face go red and she turned away. "You shouldn't be giving him ideas Margie!" she said under her breath.

When she glanced back, Bertie was looking at her with a thoughtful expression on his face. Caro's heart sank.

CHAPTER THREE

"How exactly *would* you go about stealing a diamond?" Edward pondered aloud. Caro sipped her sherry, watching her brother roll the snifter of brandy loosely between his hands. She smiled. Her mother, quietly doing needlework across the room, would have a fit if she looked up and saw her finest crystal being handled in such a cavalier fashion.

"It would be like stealing anything else, I'd wager," offered Bertie. He also had a drink in hand, and his feet up on a footstool. He leaned back into the wingback chair by the fire which popped and crackled brightly.

"First of all, you would have to be sure you weren't seen," he continued, "and you had enough time to crack the safe and then to get away. Or, on a more simple level, just snatch the stuff when the counter assistant isn't looking and make off with it, I suppose."

"The problem with that is it's messy. You're bound to leave some clue – they say you can identify someone through their fingerprints alone," Caro chimed in, placing her glass on the table beside her. "Besides, when you start in with the criminal class, you're bound to bump into some informer who will snitch on you."

Now her mother *did* look up. "Caroline! That's hardly an observation a young lady should be making!"

Edward shifted and looked over his shoulder at his mother. She held a silver needle poised above the embroidery hoop on her lap. A length of orange silk trailed from it like flame back to the needlework.

"It's just hypothetical, mother. Besides, we're interested to know how The Phantom does it. Unlike the cases in the detective stories Caro likes to read, there are no clues and no one has snitched on him yet."

"I would prefer *neither* of my children use such common language."

Bertie leaned forward and picked up the discarded newspaper by the fire. He made a show of being interested in it. Caro gave a small smile. It seemed her erstwhile beau was trying to make himself invisible.

Her mother went back to her needlework and the friends sat in silence.

After a moment, Bertie lowered the newspaper, his eyes bright. "Well, if there is one thing that will bring The Phantom out it's this: The Star of December."

Bertie read out the report.

Count Valois arrived in London today with the rarest of gems. The Star of December diamond, which once decorated the crowns of both Spanish and Bavarian kings, is to go on display in London for one day, following an invitation-only evening showing. The Count and his valuable gem will embark a national tour in the New Year.

The Star of December diamond is 35 carats in

weight and is a rare grey-blue colour with facets cut in such a way as to resemble a star.

The London showing will be by special invitation only on December 22 at the Longmuir Hotel.

"Look, they even have an illustration." Bertie turned the newspaper around. Indeed, the sketch of the diamond showed a stone with star-like points across its face.

"I hardly wish to encourage you," said Caro's mother without looking up, "but you may be in luck. Walter has been asked *personally* to arrange the security for the London showing. If you ask nicely, he might see if he can arrange for you amateur detectives to go along too."

* * *

A light dusting of snow drifted from the leaden morning sky.

Caro emerged from the book store with her latest acquisition wrapped in brown paper. The Moonstone by Wilkie Collins had just arrived and that would be her Christmas gift from her brother – if she had the patience not to read it before the day.

She held her burgundy coloured cloak closed with her free gloved hand and made her way to the intersection that would allow her to catch the horse-drawn tram back to the comfort of home.

As she approached the corner, she saw a newspaper boy raise a copy of The Standard high in his hand.

"Read all abaht it! Theft at Barrington Arcade! Diamond Butterfly floats away! Read all abaht it! The Phantom strikes again. Scotland Yard clueless ag—"

The boy stopped when he noticed Caro glower at him. She thrust a penny at him and snatched a paper from his gloved hand.

The story itself was just a few lines; a stop press for the city edition. And she hadn't misheard, it *was* the jewellery store. The very same jewellery store she had been in yesterday had been robbed!

Behind her a bell rang, announcing the arrival of a tram. She handed the conductor a threepenny bit and took a window seat, watching as the snow squalled in the increasing wind. The tram passed street after street and suddenly there was the Barrington Arcade. On a whim, Caro got off the tram at the nearby stop.

> *O star of wonder, star of night,*
> *Star with royal beauty bright,*
> *Westward leading, still proceeding,*
> *Guide us to thy perfect light.*

She was barely aware of the carollers as she rushed into the arcade, dodging shoppers focused on completing their own Christmas errands. When she reached the jewellery store, a young constable in his blue wool uniform and boss-topped custodian helmet was at the door trying to look as intimidating as possible to ward off a small throng of onlookers.

The blinds were down on all of the windows, preventing anyone from looking in.

Among the crowd, two shifty-looking men – reporters Caro guessed – began to remonstrate with each other and the constable stepped forward to intervene. Caro saw her opportunity. She slipped around one of the decorated potted conifers and through the door which, to her good fortune, had been left ajar which meant the bell did not ring as she entered.

The shop was unoccupied and the door to the workshop beyond was open. She heard voices, including one she identified as her Uncle's.

Caro didn't call out. She recalled her conversation with Uncle Walter about observation and looked about.

The shop itself appeared almost exactly as it did yesterday, except there was now a cloth over the glass counter and, behind her, the window display was different. She cast her eyes over it. Some of the more expensive items were missing. She tried to recall what she'd seen yesterday that was now missing - a gold sovereign case, a silver tea service, and a suite of jewellery – earbobs, choker and bracelet set with emeralds. Oh – and an exquisite pocket watch, gone too.

But the windows were intact. The shop was neat and tidy, so there had been nothing ransacked. Had the door been jimmied?

It stood ajar still, just as Caro left it after slipping inside. She approached cautiously to examine it, not wanting to alert the young policeman outside. She got a momentary glance at the lock before–

Slam! Jingle, jingle, jingle!

The constable outside, ignorant of her presence right behind the door, pulled it closed and the bell tinkled brightly. A moment later, Caro sensed someone behind her.

"I hope they teach in those law classes that obstruction of a police officer is a criminal offence."

Caro ignored Uncle Walter's gruffness and turned around with a ready smile she knew always won him over.

"I'm not obstructing anything. In fact I could be a witness."

He raised an eyebrow in surprise.

"I doubt that very much," he said but Caro heard the annoyance in his voice leach away.

"Inspector? Did you say something?" A voice called from the other room then a face appeared around the corner. Caro barely recognised the policeman who had been at her door two days earlier without the scarf obscuring his face.

Walter sighed.

"Caro, this is my Sergeant, Bill Parkes. Parkes, this is my niece and amateur detective Caroline Addison. She's studying law."

Caro couldn't tell whether that tidbit of information impressed the sergeant or not. Now introductions had been made, Parkes disappeared back into the workshop.

"Well, now you're here and not likely to go away, you may as well see what's going on. It will be something to share with your college chums after the Christmas break," he said.

"The papers are saying it was the work of The Phantom."

"They *would*," Walter harrumphed. "According to the jeweller, the brooch was locked in the safe, along with the most valuable of the window display items at seven o'clock when the shop closed for the evening. Hargreaves and his assistant were here until ten o'clock finishing up a commissioned piece for a customer. They swept the floors, locked the connecting door, and then the front door which was checked by each and every beadle at the beginning of his rounds and again before he went off shift."

Walter started towards the workshop then halted. "Does your father know you're here?"

Caro shook her head.

"I thought not... Well, don't touch anything."

Caro kept a hold of her book instead and followed.

The workshop behind was only as large as the shop front. Two benches ran the length of each side wall. One bench had a small lathe on it. Various probes, clamps and other bits of equipment in brass, which Caro couldn't identify, were placed neatly in an open box. It looked like a dentist's surgery right down to a magnifying glass clamped to the table.

The safe stood large against the back wall, flanked by bespoke cabinets.

"Mr Hargreaves went through everything again, sir," Parkes said. "Nothing is missing apart from the butterfly brooch."

"There doesn't seem to be any signs of forced entry. I looked for scratches on the front door lock," said Caro.

Parkes glanced at her then to Walter, who gave him a slight nod.

"No, miss," he said, somewhat reluctantly in Caro's opinion. "The owner had no idea anything was out of order until he started setting up for work this morning."

"The newspaper said..."

"Newspapers *lie*, miss. We have men from The Argus, The Illustrated News and The Standard all waiting outside. It doesn't matter what we tell them, they just make it up to sell more papers."

"That's enough, Parkes," said the Inspector, and Caro looked away to spare the sergeant some of the embarrassment of being chipped by his superior in front of her. Looking down, she noticed some sawdust on the floor. The apprentice who'd swept up at the end of the day seemed to be a little haphazard in his duties. Their housekeeper at home would have a fit if one of her girls had missed a single mote.

"Shall we see if we can find some fingerprints on the safe?" said her uncle.

Caro's head rose. "I've heard of this! I had no idea Scotland Yard was using the technique."

"I thought it was worth a try, but I'm not very hopeful."

"Why not?" Caro frowned, recalling some reading she had done. "Sir Francis Galton says classification of fingerprints could be useful in identifying an individual."

Walter patted his coat pocket, perhaps looking for his pipe. After a moment he gave up and answered her question. "The thief who goes to this amount of planning to steal one specific jewel and get out again without anyone being the wiser is a clever man, a cautious one who wouldn't leave anything to chance. Someone *that* clever has probably read Galton – and would wear gloves."

"So how *did* he get in?"

"If we knew the answer to that, then we'd be closer to getting him."

Walter told the jeweller he could open up in front while they finished in the back room. Hargreaves and his assistant moved past them. Parkes sniffed.

"If you ask me, to get away with this a man would have to be a ruddy magician—" He halted suddenly remembering his manners. "—pardon, Miss Addison."

* * *

Caro thought about the sergeant's remark as she left the arcade and waited for the tram to take her near home. A gust of wind tugged at a coloured handbill posted on a pillar beside the Tudor Inn cake emporium.

THE PALLADIAN THEATRE

Thrills and Delights

Direct from The Continent

Acrobats & Jugglers

Also featuring

THE DARK DUKE

Magician Extraordinaire!

Across the face of it another piece of paper had been glued:

LAST DAYS

She paused to look at the theatre opposite.

Yes, it would take a ruddy magician indeed!

CHAPTER FOUR

T he Gilfroy Winter Ball had always been one of the highlights of the season, and this year's was no exception.

Caro felt Bertie's hand on her back, urging her through the throng. Although it was still early, the place was packed with revellers.

"Eddie and I were told by the youngest Gilfroy we were all in for something special – the old man has gone all out this year," he said.

The doors in the entrance hall were open wide this evening, offering a tantalising glimpse of the grand ballroom beyond decked out in red and gold stripes. The dancing guests swirling about in their formal gowns were dressed no less colourfully.

In fact, everyone was clad in their finest. Caro wore a gown of vibrant red. Setting off Gwen's dark hair was her gown of emerald green; Margaret dressed in peach.

Caro glanced back to make sure they were all together. She gave Margaret a squeeze of her hand, while Edward tucked Gwen's arm in his and whistled low. "I thought the young sprat was exaggerating when he said they were doing something inspired by Blackpool's Winter Gardens but, by George, he's done it!"

"Dancing first?" Bertie enquired.

"Look!" Margaret pointed up to the portrait gallery on the second floor. "There are jugglers up there."

"I think I can see a coconut shie," Caro added with enthusiasm.

Bertie shrugged his shoulders.

"Upstairs first it is, ladies."

* * *

Tonight the portraits were hidden away, made safe for the gallery to be transformed into a carnivalesque side show. Edward showed his prowess, managing to ring the bell in the strong man game and won Gwen a toy monkey. Bertie was a much better shot at the coconut shie than Caro, but she proved to have a good eye for the hoopla ring toss.

They stopped to watch the tumblers, two men dressed in fitted white and black costumes. First, they expertly wielded clubs, tossing one, then two spinning high into the upper void of the gallery and deftly catching them before they fell to the polished timber floors. Then they performed a series of acrobatic tumbles and tosses, back flips and leaps – all to the delight of the watching guests.

After exhausting all the amusements upstairs, Caro and her friends returned to the ground floor. At a distance Caro saw her parents talking to their hosts in the ballroom. Lady Constance was wearing a magnificent suite of heirloom diamonds and her gown in gold brocade was designed to show them off. The necklace was more like a collar around her throat and the bracelet at her wrist was nearly as wide. The earrings themselves featured individual brilliant diamonds as big as thumbnails.

Bertie leaned in between Caro and Margaret. He threw his arm around Gwen to include her in the conversation. "What do you think, ladies?" he asked sotto voce. "Do you think The Phantom will show tonight to collect his haul?"

"With everyone who is here tonight – including the Chief Inspector of Scotland Yard?" said Caro. "He'd be foolish if he tried."

"I wonder if they're real," said Margaret. "I mean, they could very well be paste. I think I'd be too frightened to wear anything *that* expensive."

"They only come out for special occasions like this one," offered Gwen. "They are said to have belonged to Catherine The Great and were Sir Hubert's wedding gift to his second wife."

Bertie tapped Caro on the shoulder and drew her away so as not to be overheard.

"Speaking of which... Caro, I need to have a word with you. Would it convenient for me to call on you tomorrow?"

Caro found herself frozen in place. *A proposal!* She was sure of it! *Oh, Bertie...* How on earth was she going to let her poor friend down gently? She could think of no good excuse at the present.

"Um, yes, ah, I'm sure that will be fine."

At Bertie's delighted look, Caro felt even worse.

Dancing was always the best way to revive battered spirits and Caro threw herself into it with gusto.

She danced with her brother – when she could tear him away from Gwen. What a lovely couple Edward and Gwen made, she thought with great affection. Gwen seemed already part of the family although the wedding wasn't until early spring.

The thought made her soften towards Bertie and she accepted an invitation to dance with him. He really was a sweet fellow who made her laugh with his witty observations about the other guests as they glided about the room.

That was just the awful thing – she loved him nearly as much as her brother and in much the same way. The thought of being anything more to him just didn't feel right. She dreaded what her mother would say if she refused his proposal. Ah, maman... she didn't always see eye to eye with her, but she knew her mother meant well – to see her daughter happily married... what mother didn't want that for her daughter?

Well, there was no point thinking about it tonight – *tomorrow brings its own troubles*.

"Those icicles thawed quickly," said Bertie, tilting his head over to Caro's right.

"Hmmm?"

"Her diamond jewellery, she's no longer wearing it."

Bertie pivoted on his front foot. Caro spun with him, seeing for herself that the elaborate suite of gems no longer hung around Lady Constance's neck.

"That *was* quick," she agreed. "I wonder why?"

The music came to an end. The dancers stopped and applauded each other and the band. Bertie escorted Caro from the floor towards two vacant chairs. He attracted the attention of a passing footman and retrieved two glasses of punch, handing the first to Caro.

"I overheard Sir Hubert on my way back to the ballroom after a cigar." Bertie paused to slake his thirst. "He was worried about her losing it, the necklace, I think... something about the clasp being loose."

"Well, at least it will be safe and secure. Uncle Walter won't have to have his men trail the Gilfroys all evening."

Bertie drained his drink.

"Another dance?" he asked.

Caro shook her head. "I think I might join Gwen and Edward in the drawing room. The Dark Duke is supposed to be making an appearance tonight."

"I *see*."

Caro sharpened her glare at Bertie's teasing tone.

"Oh, don't give me give me that look," he continued with a grin. "All the way home from that performance, you and Margaret talked about how handsome he was – and the estimable Gwen too. It was all enough to make a chap feel quite inadequate."

She took the banter in the spirit in which it was meant – she knew Bertie too well to take it any other way. She rose and tapped him on the arm with her fan and directed his attention to where Margaret had just returned from the dance floor on the arm of the eligible Viscount Scottsdale.

"Well, practice your wooing skills on Margaret over there and not me," she said, slightly surprised to see his smile dim a little at her words. She had no idea she had wounded him that much. She attempted to take the sting out of them by patting his arm.

"Friends?"

He placed a hand over her hand and gave it a light squeeze, and an even tighter smile.

"Go on, enjoy the magician and I'll call on you tomorrow afternoon."

* * *

The conservatory, which ran the southern length of Gilfroy Hall, had been turned into a tea room and decorated in calming white, soft blue and green for the ball. It was well-heated for the benefit of the tropical plants, as much as the comfort for the guests, and it proved to be a peaceful respite from the noise and activity in the ballroom and the picture gallery. A harpist sat in the corner and played softly – just enough to be heard over the hubbub of voices.

Moving among the guests was a tall man. At first Caro thought he might be a footman as he approached one table and bowed, but he carried himself too assuredly. Here was The Dark Duke.

When he turned, Caro noted the waistcoat he wore over a crisp white shirt was finely tailored. The front was an exquisite wine red silk, embroidered in gold thread; at his throat was a black cravat folded over just the once and held in place with a single diamond stud. It took a confident man to wear such an ensemble.

Caro found Gwen and Edward seated at a small round table near a topiary bush where soft white flowers studded the dark green foliage. As she approached, she detected the sweet creamy scent of the gardenia flowers.

Behind her was the sound of laughter and enthusiastic applause.

"Enjoying yourself, Caro?" Gwen asked. She moved the toy monkey and patted the empty seat beside her.

"Sir Hubert has certainly outdone himself this year," Caro agreed. "This must have cost a small fortune.

Edward set down his coffee cup.

"I'm glad that's finally put the rumours to rest. According to gossips in the City—"

Gwen grinned and picked up her tea cup. "And here I thought only women gossiped..."

Caro grinned. Edward gave them both a meaningful look before he continued, leaning in conspiratorially.

"Over the past few months Sir Hubert has divested himself of a large number of shares on the exchange. Now that could mean nothing – he may want to increase his cash liquidity for any number of reasons – a new business acquisition for instance, but people *are* talking..."

"And *I* think it's rude to be talking about our host while we're guests in his home," Gwen chided.

Edward tilted his head in acknowledgement.

Gwen nudged her. "We've been waiting for The Dark Duke to come to our table. We've been watching him perform tricks for guests at the other tables. Eddie thinks he'll be able to figure them out if he sees them up close. I just want to look at *him* up close – just to see if he is as handsome as Margaret claims. Oh, here he comes now."

CHAPTER FIVE

Caro drew breath as the man approached. He was even better looking up close. His dark hair was smartly cut. His eyes, a grey so pale as to be colourless, were mesmerising enough without any conjuring he might do.

He bowed.

"Ladies and gentleman, my name is Tobias Black. I am The Dark Duke."

He performed a flourish with his hands. When they stilled, there was a calling card between his index and middle fingers. Black placed it on the table and pulled a deck of playing cards from his trouser pocket.

"I'm here this evening to tell you that everything is an illusion," he said, shuffling the cards. "The mind sees what it wants to see. The facts are a matter of interpretation."

He turned the deck so the short side faced them and used his thumb to flick through the cards. He did this several times before turning to Gwen.

"Did you see a card of interest, miss?"

Black flicked through the deck once again.

"No, don't tell me," he warned, raising a finger. Black put the deck back in his pocket and pulled out a card.

"I know it's not this one," he said, showing the Seven of Clubs. "Is it... this one?"

Black flicked the top corner of the Seven of Clubs and it transformed into the Queen of Diamonds. Caro could tell by the look on Gwen's face that indeed it was the card she had chosen. In fact, that had been the card she had silently picked herself.

The magician turned to Edward. "I see you're looking perplexed."

"I'm trying to work out how you did that."

Black grinned.

"Perhaps the magic isn't with me, perhaps..." he turned swiftly to Caro, "it's with you."

"Me?"

"Uh-hmm. I can tell there is something very special about you."

Caro fought a blush and Black produced the deck of cards once more. He fanned them so only the backs and not the suits were on view.

"Take one."

Caro found a card at her fingertips. She glanced at it. The Jack of Hearts. She showed the card to Gwen and Edward and handed it face up into Black's outstretched hand.

"Ah..." he said as he examined the card. "I think this could be love! The Knave of Hearts wishes to bend his knee to the lovely lady. All you have to do is wave your fingers and he will go weak at the knees. Go on."

Caro felt foolish, wiggling her fingers at a simple playing card. But it moved!

She watched it, fascinated, as it undulated like a belly dancer. She felt her eyes widen and, when she looked up to Black, he smiled at her – not a polite upturn of the lips but a full smile that caused little butterflies in her stomach to take wing.

Gwen and Edward applauded.

"And before I take my leave of you; one more trick for your amusement." Black pulled another card from his pocket – the Nine of Spades. He flicked it one way and then another presumably to show it was just an ordinary card. He rested it in the palm of his hand.

"Things which are seemingly impossible, *are* possible," he said, placing his other hand six inches above the one holding the card. He waved the upper hand and the card in the lower one started to move.

The card moved again and then appeared to be levitating in Black's hand, before it lowered to rest in his palm once more. The magician leaned forward to pick up the teaspoon resting by Gwen's tea cup. He waved the spoon over the top of the card. A moment later it moved again, rising to sit above his hand.

"You see, no strings."

Now he inserted the spoon sideways between the card and his palm. The card seemed to hover over the spoon. The friends gasped in disbelief.

"Illusion is the first of all pleasures," said The Dark Duke.

Caro recognised the quote. "Voltaire," she said and was rewarded with another of his full smiles and a tilt of his head in acknowledgement. He put the spoon back on the table and returned the playing card to his pocket.

"Remind me never to play bridge against you," Edward quipped, joining in Gwen and Caro's applause.

Black bowed once more and turned away to approach another table. Caro reached for The Dark Duke's card and saw three theatre tickets, which most certainly had not been there when he placed the business card on the table.

For the next half an hour, she pretended involvement in Gwen and Edward's conversation while she watched the magician perform sleight of hand for other guests. As far as she could tell, Tobias Black didn't use the same set of tricks at each table. At one she saw the flash of a silver coin, at another he used a red silk kerchief and at a third the deck of cards made another appearance.

She observed as he stopped to speak to the harpist and they left together through the servant's door.

"Well?" Caro asked.

"Well what?" answered Edward, frowning with confusion.

"Did you work out how he did those tricks?"

Edward shook his head slowly. "Not a clue, but one thing's for certain – between him and The Phantom, they could make the Crown Jewels disappear!"

"You're not saying—" Caro started.

Gwen shook her head. "I'm sure Edward was only joking."

Caro wished *she* could be so certain.

A man would have to be a ruddy magician...

* * *

Caro closed her eyes against a slight headache and rolled her silk stockings down her legs. It was late and she was glad her family had accepted Sir Hubert's invitation to stay in the guest wing.

In the hall the grandfather clock struck two and even at this hour, she could hear the sound of people leaving the house. Lingering guests? Perhaps they were staff hired for the evening or maybe the entertainers.

Regardless, the permanent household servants would have their work cut out for them to bring the residence back to order before the master and mistress of the house rose for brunch.

Gwen was preparing for bed on the other side of the room, softly humming to herself as she brushed her hair.

"How did you know my brother was *the one*?" Caro asked.

"The one what?"

Caro laid the stockings over the chair beside the bed and climbed between the sheets. "You know, the one you wanted to spend the rest of your life with."

There was a long pause. Gwen watched her through the reflection in the dressing table mirror.

"There were lots of different reasons," Gwen said and took up brushing her hair once more. "And, thinking about it, none of them would make sense to anyone else. I think you *know* when you know. But I take it that's not the answer you're looking for?"

Caro shrugged and settled her head back into the pillow.

Gwen left the dressing table and turned back the covers of her bed. She extinguished the gas lamp on the wall near her bed, throwing the room into darkness.

As Caro heard her getting into bed, Gwen also spoke. "Is there anyone in particular you're thinking of?"

"No, not really…" Caro answered, knowing it wasn't really the truth. She closed her eyes, but she was almost too tired to sleep. She didn't like to think of Bertie being a problem, but his misplaced affections had to be dealt with soon.

* * *

A scream pierced the silence. A moment later, footsteps ran down the hall.

By the time Gwen had lit the candle, the noises had stopped, but Caro was already up, putting on a dressing gown.

She opened the door to look down the passageway. The end of it was as well-lit as though it was already past dawn. A fearful looking maid scurried past.

"What's happened?"

The young woman stopped.

"Oh Miss, it's the Mistress's jewellery. The Phantom 'as made off with it!"

Caro's heart plummeted. She drew a deep breath.

"Go and fetch Inspector Addison. His room is on the floor above this one," she told the visibly upset girl.

Glancing back at Gwen standing in the doorway, Caro hurried along the passageway and girded her courage to knock at the master bedroom door. Inside, she was greeted by the sight of an ashen faced Sir Hubert holding his distraught wife.

"Sir Hubert, Lady Constance," she said. "I've sent the maid for my Uncle. Is it...?"

After an awkward pause in which the couple merely gaped at her, Caro crossed the threshold into the dressing chamber. On the floor at the foot of a wall lay a painting, its gilt frame broken. The open mouth of the safe above, with the two side-by-side picture hooks that had supported the heavy frame, gave every appearance the wall itself was in shock.

Arriving beside her, Gwen gasped and Caro, following her gaze, suddenly saw what she saw – jewellery trays strewn across the floor and a hole where one of the windowpanes had been smashed.

Sir Hubert seemed to gather himself together at the sound of hurrying footsteps, then Uncle Walter entered.

The Inspector calmly put his empty pipe in his mouth and surveyed the room. Caro stood stock still, feeling all of ten years old, hoping he wouldn't see her, hoping he wouldn't send her away.

She watched him take in the safe and step around the broken painting before heading for the second storey window. He looked at the floor before it, then opened the window and looked down.

"Well?" Sir Hubert thundered. Her uncle may have been calm, but the peer had built up a significant head of steam.

"What the devil are you doing to catch this... this... this *thief* who is a menace to every decent man in this city?"

CHAPTER SIX

Caro looked out at the fog filled landscape. It was blurred and indistinct, made more so by the speed of the train as it chuffed towards the centre of the city. Her eyes itched and ached through lack of sleep.

When she blinked, her lids were heavy, yet she knew it was important to be here today. She felt it in her bones, an instinct she couldn't describe to herself, let alone to the rest of her family, so she called on Margaret and convinced her friend she had an urgent need to do more Christmas shopping.

Margaret sat beside her with today's paper in hand reading about the robbery that had taken the shine off the Gilfroy's Christmas gala. Caro had already seen the story and it was surprisingly accurate – for The Argus. Even so, it didn't quite capture what it was like to be there in person...

Uncle Walter had reacted not a jot to Sir Hubert's angry invective. He continued to chew the stem of his pipe and look around the room.

When Sir Hubert's storm of anger abated, Walter calmly asked a maid who hovered outside the door to prepare a new room for the master and mistress before he addressed the butler beside her, telling him to send one of the footmen down to the Yard.

With quiet authority, Walter ordered everyone from the room, but as she had passed, Caro felt his hand on her arm, so she stayed.

"Your thoughts?"

The question had surprised her. Walter Addison was a Detective Chief Inspector of Scotland Yard and he was asking her?

The surprise must have been evident on her face because he went on to explain. "Remember we spoke about the difference between seeing and observing? Now is the time to find how much you've learned. You were at the crime scene at the jewellery store at the Barrington Arcade. Tell me, what do you see now?"

Caro drew a deep breath and looked about once more. Uncle Walter withdrew his tobacco pouch from his dressing robe pocket and began to pack his pipe as she spoke.

"The room is in disarray and the safe is open. The picture which would have hidden the safe is on the floor and the frame is broken. Sir Hubert would need to give an itemised account, but I suspect more than just Catherine The Great's diamonds are missing because there are empty jewellery trays scattered on the floor between the safe and the window, and..."

She turned to where the curtain flapped as if calling for attention and felt the cold wind on her face.

"...the window is broken."

"Now tell me what you recall of the jewellery store robbery," said Walter, returning the pouch to his pocket.

Caro thought hard, frowning as she tried to bring those details to mind.

"The workshop was neat a... and the jeweller said the safe was locked as usual when he came in. Nothing out of place. And only one piece of jewellery was missing."

Walter nodded. "Conclusion?"

"This crime," she said, glancing back across the disarray in the Gilfroy's bedroom, "may not have been committed by The Phantom."

The pipe went back into Uncle Walter's mouth and he patted his chest, dipping his hand into his dressing robe breast pocket to pull out a box of matches. He lit his pipe and curls of blue smoke rose and were tugged away by the cold air swirling about the room.

"So what happens now?" she asked as the silence in the master bedroom stretched out.

"Well, unlike detective stories, the search for evidence is slow and painstaking. The boys will be around at first light to search for clues both in this room and in the grounds."

"What are you going to do?"

"Get some sleep, of course. It's going to be a long day tomorrow..."

The train carriage lurched. The view from the windows went black as it entered the Underground and slowed for its approach into the station.

"We're not really going shopping, are we?"

Caro looked up to find Margaret folding the newspaper and putting it on the empty seat beside her. Her expression was a mixture of annoyance and curiosity.

"Not entirely," she confessed. "I'm going to see The Dark Duke and I needed someone to come with me. I was intending to ask after lunch if you would accompany me."

Margaret folded her arms the same way she had folded the newspaper, slow and careful. Caro found herself holding her breath, waiting for her friend's verdict.

"Before I make a decision, would you mind telling me why?"

* * *

The door closed behind them, shutting out the December wind and rain. It was eerily quiet in the Palladian.

"Please tell me Tobias Black knows we're coming."

Margaret's voice echoed through the empty foyer which, in a few hours time, would be teeming with patrons. Caro decided not to reply; Margaret's long-suffering sigh told her she had worked out the answer for herself.

"You don't think he's the—"

"Shhhh! Of course I don't," Caro continued, little above a whisper. "Well, maybe... I don't know. All I know is it takes some pretty sneaky tricks to break into a jewellery store without leaving a clue."

"But from what you told me of the Gilfroys, the bedroom was virtually ransacked."

"But The Dark Duke was at the Gilfroy's party. I just want to talk to him about his magic and see if I can – I don't know, get some *sense* of what he's really like."

"Someone should knock some sense into you," Margaret grumbled.

"You don't have to stay if you don't want to."

"Oh no. Hare-brained this may be, but I'm not letting you go in alone."

Caro reached for Margaret's hands and squeezed them.

"You're the very best friend a girl could have."

The look Margaret gave her suggested that, at this moment, the compliment would not be reciprocated.

Caro approached the doors to the auditorium. They were heavy, much heavier than she'd imagined, and she could only open them wide enough to slip through sideways. The venue was in near darkness but for the footlights illuminating the stage floor.

Bang!

The sound of a door slamming somewhere off stage made Margaret jump. Caro's heart pounded in her chest but she gathered her courage and walked down the left hand aisle. As she approached, there were more sounds from backstage – banging, hammering, the scrape of something heavy being moved across the floor.

There were voices here too, but muffled and indistinct.

She looked to Margaret who kept her reticule close to her side.

"Don't look at me," she told Caro, shaking her head. "This was your idea."

Caro positioned herself at the bottom of the ten steps at the side of the stage that would take her up to the platform.

"Hello!" she called and was pleased to find her voice didn't waver. The noise behind the thick claret-coloured curtain stopped for a moment and then continued unabated. With a quick glance back to Margaret, Caro started the climb.

The footlights were like little furnaces, they warmed her ankles as she passed.

"Hello?"

With more confidence than she felt, Caro moved to centre stage to where she imagined the curtain parting to be. Margaret, having followed her up the stairs, remained on the wing.

There were more sounds behind the curtain. Caro grabbed a fistful of it and tugged.

First came the sound of a deep clang from behind her, then, as she turned, the light of a thousand suns pinned her to the heavy drape. She could barely see the auditorium seating and raised a hand to her brow to block the glare.

Blinded by the spot lamp, Caro blinked rapidly and slipped through the gap in the curtain with a couple of stumbling steps before she was encircled in strong arms and hauled up against a hard, muscular body.

"Watch your step there. The first is a big one."

Still blinded by the spot lamp, she recognised the voice nonetheless.

It was Tobias Black, the Dark Duke himself.

CHAPTER SEVEN

C aro's vision began to clear. She took a deep breath and detected the tang of neroli and rosemary as well as bitter coffee about the man who held her.

She remained in his arms and stumbled after him for a couple of steps before he released her.

The theatre curtains had been drawn wide open during her confusion and the entire stage was in view – including the equally wide open trap door she had missed by inches.

And five pairs of eyes looked at her. Six, if she included Margaret, who stood to one side ashen-faced. Beyond the trap door, a box like an upright casket painted in red and white stripes stood next to the group of surprised stage hands.

Black addressed the men.

"Back to work, everyone. We have a final show to put on and rehearsal is in two hours."

Black was not dressed as he was last night. He wore only a shirt of soft cotton – Caro's fingers could still recall the feel of it – and a pair of black trousers over boots. But it was his eyes she remembered most of all.

She was deciding what colour to call them, grey... no, that seemed too pedestrian. Pewter, perhaps? Then the eyes changed colour like quicksilver.

"Do I know you?"

She found herself without a voice for the moment.

"From the winter ball at the Gilfroy residence," he said in answer to his own question. "Am I correct?"

Caro found her words and they tumbled out one after the other.

"That is correct, Mr Black. It is important I speak to you on a matter of some importance."

One of the crew coughed and another shuffled his feet. Black stepped forward. He placed a hand on Caro's shoulder.

"Shall we have this conversation somewhere more private, ladies?"

He walked to the back of the stage and swept through a black curtain. Caro and Margaret followed. Caro had never seen the backstage of a theatre before. Thick ropes tied to large cleats kept suspended scenery aloft. On the floor around them were tea chests, papier mache rocks, and thin sheets of wood on which was painted blue-green cresting waves, their tips painted white. A discarded sign on its side read:

The Tempest
William Shakespeare
New Season in the New Year

She and Margaret were directed to a disorderly collection of chairs huddled together in one corner.

He sat down and gestured to them to sit on two chairs opposite him.

"So, what is this matter of some importance?" Black asked once they had settled. Caro was sure she heard amusement in the question.

"It has to do with your magic tricks, and particularly the disappearing act with the box."

His amusement bloomed into a fully fledged smile. "My brother magicians would excoriate me if I revealed the secrets of my tricks. But I think you've gathered how the disappearing man illusion works."

"The trap door in the floor of the stage."

Black spread his arms wide as though she had applauded, instead of merely guessing the secret.

"But that's not what you came to talk to me about is it... Miss *Addison*."

Caro gasped, or it might have been Margaret, she couldn't tell. She felt the heat rise up her face.

"I don't believe I told you my name."

"I don't believe you did either. Someone pointed out Detective Chief Inspector Walter Addison from Scotland Yard to me last night and you were talking to him. The family resemblance is quite strong. Daughter?"

"Niece."

"Ah."

There was silence again for a moment in which Caro started to lose her nerve. She flicked her eyes to Margaret. There was no sign of nervousness in her, apart from her purse clutched tight, the silk of which was creased where she had dug her nails in.

It was only for a moment or two but it seemed like an eternity before the magician's expression changed as though he had been struck by a great revelation.

"You think I'm The Phantom!"

Instead of being indignant, the man seemed delighted and Caro wasn't sure which of the two reactions might have annoyed her more.

"I think no such thing!"

Yes, well, *that* was a lie and she crossed her fingers when she said it. Worse, she could tell by the expression on his handsome face that he knew she was lying too. His next question was serious.

"Then ask me your question. What do you want to know?"

Something happened in that moment. Something unexplained. Caro felt a quickening, a strange elation. She had to gather her thoughts before speaking.

"How *does* someone disappear into thin air? Assuming they don't have a box and a hole in the stage floor," she asked.

"I told you the truth last night, Miss Addison. All magic is illusion and misdirection, nothing more. There is nothing supernatural about it. The art of magic is knowing your audience, and knowing the reaction you want from them – surprise, joy, fear, amusement – all of which are in the power of the mind."

Tobias pulled a pack of playing cards from his pocket and searched for one in particular. He found it. It was the Jack of Hearts and – without the hocus pocus of wiggling fingers and magic words – the card bent and danced all on its own.

"I want you to believe you can make a card dance, so I make it dance for you... with a little help."

He turned the card over and with a thumbnail flicked a tab made of the same backing as the playing card. Even up close the addition was difficult to see. Tobias placed the card on his lap and pulled out a deck of cards. He flicked the edge of the deck of cards towards them. Each time the Queen of Hearts stood out.

"I want you to think I can read your mind, but in reality..."

Tobias split the deck and showed them the Queen of Hearts and then the other half of the deck. The card that had been just *before* the Queen of Hearts was fully a third shorter than the rest of the cards. He put the pack together and flicked through the deck once more.

"I make you see what you *want* to see. I suspect The Phantom does the same."

"You mean his crime scenes are illusions?" Margaret asked. Tobias gave her a smile and Caro wished oddly that its brightness shone on her too.

"I think so. From what I read in the newspapers... no sign of entry or departure?" he asked. Caro confirmed it with a nod. "That tells me he's creating an illusion of invulnerability. But it *is* an illusion. A trick. He wants to force the attention of the police away from something else – in the same way a magician will use a gesture or an action to distract you."

"Find out what that is *then* you will find his sleight of hand and *that* will be his vulnerability."

Tobias stood.

"Now, if I've sated your curiosity, I'll take my leave of you. My crew and I have our last show this evening."

Caro rose and Margaret did also. Tobias took Margaret's hand and bowed over it then released it. Then he took Caro's and held it. Then his eyes held hers for a moment and he dropped a kiss on the back of her hand.

"I'm so glad it was *you* who paid me a visit... instead of a representative of Scotland Yard."

"Not at all, Mr Black," she replied, her voice a little huskier than usual, "you have been more than gracious with your time."

"Call me Tobias."

He was *flirting* with her! Caro kept the smile to herself as he escorted them both to the entrance of the theatre.

"Just one more question, Mr Black," Caro asked. "You wouldn't happen to know how someone might dispose of a suite of diamonds would you?"

* * *

Caro watched Margaret wait more-or-less patiently until the waitress at the Tudor Inn had left the pot of tea and warm cinnamon buns before speaking. The little tea house was in the perfect location to see the front entrance of the Palladian and the laneway that led to the stage door.

Caro had chosen their table specifically to ensure a good view of both. But now she girded herself. Her friend did not look happy.

"Have you *quite* finished making a fool of yourself?"

Caro poured tea for both of them and used the action to let the sting from the words fade. "It was a legitimate line of enquiry."

"For a *policeman*, Caro – not a young woman dabbling in law at college until she can find herself a man to marry."

"I'm not *dabbling*. I'm taking this seriously. The game's afoot."

Margaret raised her tea cup to her lips, making sure Caro saw the roll of her eyes. A good sip of tea later, her friend shook her head.

"Then exactly what have you deduced, *Miss Holmes*?"

"That Mister Tobias Black knows more than he's telling us."

"Caro—" The warning was clear in the way Margaret drew out her name.

"In fact, he told us *exactly* how he did it."

"Weren't there lectures on the burden of proof?" exclaimed Margaret, clearly appalled. "You can't go around accusing some poor man of being the most notorious jewel thief in London."

"I know that! That's why we're waiting. We need proof."

Margaret set down her cup. It clattered harshly on the saucer. "*I* don't need proof. I'm here on false pretences, remember? I only came with you because you were too afraid to talk to him by yourself. I still have some Christmas shopping to do. Leave the poor man alone and let your Uncle deal with criminals – what?"

Caro blinked rapidly to make sure she wasn't seeing things. There, emerging from the laneway looking very furtive indeed was Tobias Black.

CHAPTER EIGHT

C aro dropped coins on the table to pay for her tea. "Where are you going? We have to catch the 3:55 and we haven't been down the High Street yet."

She ignored Margaret's call and let the cafe door slam closed behind her while she buttoned her slate grey coat. She followed Black from a discreet distance, training her eyes on him. He wore a dusky blue greatcoat and a bright chartreuse scarf, making him easy to spot in the crowd.

Wherever he was going, he was focused about it. Not once did he look back, nor did he look about. He was a man with a purpose. He did not linger to look in the shops. He ignored the Christmas displays and the carollers on the corner.

> *Once in royal David's city,*
> *Stood a lowly cattle shed,*
> *Where a mother laid her Baby,*
> *In a manger for His bed:*
> *Mary was that mother mild,*
> *Jesus Christ, her little Child.*

The second verse of the carol was snatched by the wind as she followed him through St James Park and past Buckingham Palace.

So far they had walked a mile west of Westminster. Her shoes were comfortable enough for the job but the pace he set was making her insteps ache. She gritted her teeth against the discomfort and continued on Buckingham Palace Road, tucking her violet coloured scarf around her neck to stop the blasts of cold air running down the back of her collar.

The grand Grosvenor Hotel emerged from the fog in front of her. The imposing gothic architecture rose high. The dozens of chimneys spanning its roof top belched smoke in the mission to keep the hotel's occupants warm. As she glanced up, the clock on the central pediment rang out the third hour of the afternoon.

Caro's heart pounded in her chest, and it wasn't all from the exertion.

That's where he must be meeting his contact, his – what's the word? – his fence. It was perfectly logical, she reasoned. With Victoria Station below the hotel, all the thief had to do was deliver the diamonds. His contact could pick a ticket from any one of the railway companies there, and be away back to the continent before Scotland Yard could act.

Caro glanced up. It was starting to snow again. She pressed on through the crowd, catching a flash of Black's brightly coloured scarf as he entered the station portico. A moment later she welcomed the embrace of the wide expanse of awning that sheltered passengers from the increasingly inclement weather.

She paused to see which of the entrances he favoured.

Black wasn't heading for the hotel. He veered right to enter the terminus hall.

He was heading for one of the ticket counters, but which one? She would have to get closer if she was going to follow him. Caro gathered up her courage like a hen with her wayward chicks and held it close.

She was so near! If she reached out her hand she could touch his back. The temptation to do so was enormous. But what if he were to turn around and see her? What excuse could she offer except her suspicion that he really *was* The Phantom?

How far should she follow him? He proved himself to be charming and helpful this afternoon, but she knew nothing of him except the certainty he could be dangerous too. What if he was meeting with his gang? What should she do then?

"First class single to Brighton," she heard him say. That was miles away! How on earth did he expect to get there, conduct his business and then get back for his performance?

Caro watched the yellow slip of paper pass through the ticket window. Black turned left. Caro's heart pounded.

I'm losing him!

There, the bright green scarf! She saw him descending the stairs down to the platform.

"One platform ticket please, the Brighton line," she said without looking at the man in the booth.

Caro passed over a halfpenny, grabbed the ticket and hurried after him.

The sounds were loud here, with passengers embarking and disembarking, the chuffing plumes of smoke and vapour, the piercing sound of the whistle as boilers on the monstrous locomotives built up a head of steam. A train had just arrived on the platform. She was pressed against a tide of humanity ascending the stairs. Between shoulders and hats she could see he was already on the platform. She *had* to reach him.

Caro finally obtained the last step and pushed her way through. Equal numbers of people were now embarking on to the train bound for Brighton. Caro stood on tip toes, looking for the distinctive scarf.

A loud sharp whistle sounded to her left. Caro winced, putting a hand to her ear. The ringing stopped, replaced by the sound of the train screeching and huffing its way from the station. As it picked up speed, Caro wondered whether she'd caught a flash of green on one of the passengers on board or whether it was simply the light from the signal box reflected in the carriage window.

She walked from one end of the platform to the other and felt the crushing disappointment of defeat. She had lost him. The one clue she had, and she lost it. Her sympathy with her uncle grew exponentially. Sleuthing was a lot more exhausting than the detective novels made it out to be.

By now, the platform was nearly deserted. Porters rested against their trolleys, smoking cigarettes and enjoying a few minutes respite before the madness started all over again with the arrival of the next train.

There was nothing more for it. Caro would have to go back home and explain her strange behaviour to Margaret -- and potentially worse still, her parents. The clock on the platform showed twenty minutes to four and Caro had the niggling feeling there was somewhere she had to be at that hour but for the life of her she couldn't remember what it was.

Rather than trudging the two miles back in dark, dank conditions on the street, she decided the wisest thing to do would be to take the train back to Charing Cross. Feeling somewhat dispirited after her adventure, she turned to trudge up the stairs when something at the foot of the stairs beside a rubbish bin caught her eye.

She looked about to ensure she was unobserved before dipping down and picking it up.

It was a chartreuse coloured scarf.

* * *

The day had turned to black by the time she reached New Scotland Yard located on the Victoria Embankment. The lamp lighters had done their work and the dirty yellow streetlamps glowed valiantly against the gloom. It was enough to illuminate the banded red brick and white Portland stone building ahead.

A large blue lamp glowed showing the entrance to the police station. Caro patted the scarf which she had stuffed into the long pocket of her coat and entered. She drew near to the counter and an expression of caution crossed the face of the sergeant on duty. The middle-aged man looked her up and down. Caro supposed he was deciding whether she was villain or victim.

"My name is Caroline Addison. I'd like to see Detective Inspector Walter Addison, please."

The man frowned and rubbed his whiskers.

"I'm his niece," she prompted.

That elicited a reaction. The sergeant turned to a bank of speaking tubes on the wall behind. He picked up one of the black hoses and blew a whistle attached to the brass trumpet at the end of the hose. A few moments later, a muffled voice emerged from the contraption.

The sergeant threw a glance over his shoulder before speaking into the device. Then he put it to his ear to it and listened, and nodded before hanging up the tube on its brass hook.

"Wait here," he said to Caro. He turned his attention to a large ledger and proceeded to completely ignore her presence.

A few moments later she heard the sound of booted feet descending two at a time on a staircase hidden behind two large oak doors.

When they opened, Caro was not at all surprised to see a young, fresh faced constable.

The sergeant didn't bother to look up.

"Take the young miss here up to see Chief Inspector Addison, Jenkins."

"Follow me, Miss," the young man instructed.

And she duly did, to the first floor and then along a corridor with offices either side. In each door was a glass panel painted with the name of its occupant. Some of these rooms were dark, their doors closed, the staff out for the afternoon.

She followed Constable Jenkins to an office where the light shone brightly. The door was ajar. She waited to one side as the constable knocked on the door and announced her presence from the doorway.

He stood aside and Caro took that as an invitation to enter.

"Uncle, thank you for seeing me," she said, even as she passed through the doorway and strode up to his desk. "I know this is highly unusual, but I need to tell you something; something about The Phantom case."

Uncle Walter sat behind his desk, but he had an odd expression on his face. She was about to ask him about it when she observed he was not alone.

Lounging rather comfortably on an upholstered chair to one side of the office was Tobias Black.

CHAPTER NINE

C aro looked at her uncle who frowned and then back at Tobias Black who did not – instead the man gave her a Cheshire cat grin.

"It seems introductions are superfluous," Uncle Walter observed.

"Yes, we *have* met," she said before her voice trailed off.

She watched him and waited. Waited for him to tell her uncle about her questions at the theatre... waited for him to say she had accused him of being The Phantom. Her throat dried up.

Instead, he stood, stepped forward and clasped her hand for a moment.

"Miss Addison and I first met at the Gilfroy's ball, Inspector."

"Ah, yes." Uncle Walter nodded absently, now turning his attention back to Caro.

"Now what's this about important information about The Phantom?"

Caro watched Tobias's reaction carefully. He didn't seem to be nervous. Instead, his attention to her was openly curious.

What *could* she say? That she was about to accuse the man of being The Phantom himself?

Her theory had seemed sound enough. If it takes a magician to rob a locked jewellery shop and leave no trace, then she'd present Scotland Yard with a magician.

Here was a man with the means – Tobias Black was a master of sleight of hand. The motive was perfectly self-evident – those diamonds were worth a king's ransom. And the opportunity? The Barrington Arcade robbery took place overnight. The only people who could be around that late at night and not arouse suspicion were the performers at the Palladian Theatre across the road from the arcade.

It made sense. Perfect sense. She had spent a great deal of time formulating her theory. But now that the prime suspect was before her...

She prised her tongue from the arid roof of her mouth before answering.

"Sawdust."

She nearly laughed to see the comical astonishment on both men's faces. If the thought and the word had not struck her like a bolt from the blue a split second before it leapt from her mouth, she might have seen the funny side herself.

"It's been bothering me ever since we looked in the jeweller's workshop, uncle," she said.

"The apprentice claimed he swept the floor before leaving that night and yet when we were there in the morning, there was a sprinkling of sawdust all over the workroom floor.

"I've been wondering where it might have come from and I can only think of one place–"

"–The ceiling."

Caro turned to Tobias and nodded. "Yes, the ceiling. But..." She paused, frowning.

"But what?"

"I can't imagine how they did it."

"Did you look at the ceiling?"

"Umm..." Caro suddenly realised she hadn't given it a glance. The connection with the sawdust had only just come to her; how could she admit she hadn't even looked up once?

Tobias released her from her dilemma by turning immediately to Uncle Walter.

"Did you examine it, Inspector?"

"Examine it? No. It's a high ceiling. It would take a tall man on top of a six foot stepladder just to touch it. But I *did* look up at it. There were no holes cut through it."

"Can you describe it to me, Inspector?"

Walter leaned back in his chair and looked up at the plaster ceiling of his office. "A bit nicer than mine," he said. "It matched the ceiling in the shop – wooden beams and panels. What's that type called?"

"Coffered?" suggested Caro.

"Yes, that's it – it was a coffered ceiling. Oak perhaps. Dark, anyway, from the work lamps. Square panels."

Caro watched Tobias bridge his fingers together and touch his lips. His brow furrowed a moment before the expression turned to one of elation.

"Now that makes perfect sense, Inspector! Our thief breaks into the office above the jewellery store, removes some floorboards, cuts out a ceiling panel from above and lowers himself down. He opens the safe, takes the diamond butterfly and closes the safe, hauls himself up to the office, replaces the panel and leaves."

Tobias smiled at Caro. "It's a bit like a trapdoor trick, actually."

She blushed and was thankful her uncle was looking down as he packed his pipe. He nodded thoughtfully.

"That's not something to be done in one night. We'll take a closer look at that ceiling and ask the beadles on watch if they noticed anything unusual in the days prior to the robbery, trespassers on the second floor – that type of thing.

"Does that fit with the men you have under surveillance, Tobias?"

Caro frowned. "Surveillance?"

Uncle Walter smiled at her.

"I think you and Tobias need to be *properly* introduced."

"Caroline, this is Captain Tobias Black, formerly of the South Lancashire Regiment, First Battalion. He's been helping us narrow down the hunt for The Phantom for the past two weeks."

***

At the sound of the front door bell, Caro gulped down her cup of tea, nearly scalding her mouth. Considering she was far too excited to sleep last night, the pain at least ensured she was wide awake for the early morning caller.

Her mother watched her most unladylike behaviour and set down the newspaper.

"Caroline! Where are you going? You promised to help me plan the menu for Christmas dinner. *And* you missed a call from Albert yesterday. He is such a nice young man and he likes you enough to call. You need to pay attention to these things if you're ever to attract a suitor. I don't know where your mind is, my girl!"

Indeed, her mother was cross today and Caro supposed she could not blame her. There was family on Father's side coming from Wales to spend Christmas and Mother did not like them much.

Caro remembered her grumbling about the very same topic last Christmas. "Singing, they're always singing," she typically complained.

At the sound of Uncle Walter's voice in the hallway, Caro stepped around her mother's chair, placed her hands on the older woman's shoulders and kissed her on the cheek.

"I promise to call on Bertie this afternoon and apologise for missing our appointment," she said.

"Better," the older woman said, somewhat mollified.

"Ready?" asked Walter from the drawing room doorway.

Caro's mother turned to look up at her brother-in-law.

"Really, Walter, is this type of thing suitable for a young girl? Running around with ruffians and miscreants..."

"Caro is a responsible young *woman* and will be with me, Estelle. She'll be perfectly safe," he replied evenly. "Besides, with her law studies and keen eye for detail,

I might recommend the Chief Constable makes her a special deputy."

Uncle Walter winked at Caro, who could barely cover her amusement. Her mother, on the other hand, was appalled.

"Women as detectives? I never heard such a ridiculous thing in all my days. You're filling her head with nonsense," she said. "Between you and her father encouraging all sorts of strange notions, you'll spoil her for a sensible life."

At that, Uncle Walter must have decided discretion was the better part of valour when it came to his sister-in-law and he wisely elected to say nothing more.

Caro kissed her mother on the cheek once again.

"A sensible life is overrated, maman."

Her mother squeezed her arm and returned the gesture, whispering softly, "You know I only want the best for you, darling."

Caro gave her a small smile and left.

* * *

Tobias Black was talking to one of the arcade's beadles when they arrived. There was something mesmerising about Black and Caro wondered what it was. There was an air of authority he seemed to wear as comfortably as his smartly tailored coat for a start.

That he had been an Army Captain should have come as no surprise. He must have gone to the academy at Woolwich or perhaps Sandhurst College. That meant he must come from a well-to-do family. Perhaps grandmother might know them?

Caro stopped herself right there – she was beginning to sound like her mother.

In the pocket of her grey-blue coat was Tobias's scarf. She ran her fingers through it. She would return it to him when he explained how he managed to evade her at Victoria Station.

The jeweller, Mr Hargreaves, was only too pleased to let the Inspector and his party into his workshop – anything to help the police with their enquiries, particularly if it meant his showpiece diamond butterfly brooch would be returned.

Caro watched Tobias looking up at the coffered oak ceiling as a policeman stood by with the stepladder he had carried in. At length, Tobias directed the constable to stand the ladder in one spot. The constable steadied it as Tobias climbed to the top and stretched up, running a fingertip along the inside edge of the sunken panel within one coffer.

Peering up to where he touched, Caro suddenly perceived a slight line of honey-coloured oak along one edge undarkened by the years of soot from the work lamps. Tobias pushed against the centre of the panel and it lifted slightly. He let it fall back into place.

"This panel has been removed from above," he said. "It's only obvious when you're up close to it. It seems Miss Addison's theory is correct."

"But how did they do it?" Mr Hargreaves's apprentice asked.

"Good question," Tobias responded, "We're going to need access to the office upstairs to find out."

"That's the solicitors office," offered the beadle, "but they're away."

Uncle Walter turned to the man. "Have you got the keys?"

Caro followed her uncle and the beadle out of the jewellery store and onto the busy concourse. They headed to one of the marble and wrought iron staircases that would take them to the second floor where more shops mixed with professional offices.

The skylight above filtered bright winter sunshine into the space, making the Christmas decorations glitter gaily. It was strange; it was as though she was looking at the arcade through different eyes. She had only been here a week ago and then, like all of these other shoppers around her, had gone about her business blissfully unaware.

She found Tobias had fallen in step with her.

"Am I forgiven?" he asked.

She smiled in spite of herself.

"For what?" she asked, not willing to let him off the hook – not immediately, anyway.

"For sending you on a fruitless errand all the way to Victoria Station."

"You knew you were being followed?"

"Of course! I never forget a pretty face. I saw you and your friend in the cafe across the road."

"If you're not guilty, then why did you run?"

"I didn't run. I walked. Quickly. And I wanted to see how persistent you really were. If you were prepared to suspect me, you might have been tempted to ask questions of other members of the troupe working out of the Palladian."

Caro stopped on the second step of the staircase, which brought her eye to eye with Tobias who stood on the step below. She knew a question was written all over her face, but he shook his head in answer.

"Not here. Somewhere we won't be overheard."

He joined her on the second step and she felt him touch her elbow so she started to climb again, in step with him.

"I don't know how I could have lost you at the station; you're not easy to miss!" she said.

Caro watched him take her remark as a compliment but she could not detect any arrogance or ego in it.

"Remember what I said to you yesterday? Illusion is about misdirection. You weren't really following me; you were following my scarf. So all I had to do to disappear was remove it."

"As simple as that?" she breathed, recalling the moment clearly in her own mind.

"As simple as that," he confirmed with an easy smile. "And you never even saw me walk back up the stairs right past you."

They had reached midway along the gallery and joined Uncle Walter and the beadle outside an office. A small brass plaque beside the door announced its occupant:

Skeene & Roy
Solicitors

Blinds on the inside of the windows shuttered the view of the office. A handwritten sign in neat copperplate was posted on the door.

Christmas Felicitations
Our offices will be closed between
December 10 and January 7 inclusive
We wish our clients all the joy of the Season

The sound of shoppers rose up from the void. Caro crossed to the iron balustrade and looked down, estimating the distance it would take someone to get to the ground safely. Someone with a head for heights, that was for certain.

When she returned her attention to the office, she saw her uncle put his hand up to prevent the beadle from using his set of keys to open the door. Uncle Walter squatted down to look at the brass door escutcheon.

"There are fine scratch marks around the inside lip of the key hole," he announced.

"The Phantom couldn't have picked a better location and time," Tobias observed. "A skilled lock pick could be in and out quickly, and he could work inside for days and never be noticed."

Walter stood and nodded to the beadle who now used his master key to unlock the door. "Wait here," he told the man who appeared happy to obey the instruction to remain outside. To Caro's surprise, her uncle let Tobias lead the way in. She followed behind them.

Tobias took a few paces into the dim office and stopped.

"Do you smell that?"

Almost in unison, she and her uncle took in a deep breath. Caro could detect stale tobacco and musty air but little else.

"It's a pity we don't have the real Sherlock Holmes here," she said. Both men looked at her. "If there is tobacco smoke, there might be cigar or cigarette ash. Holmes wrote a monograph identifying one hundred and forty types of ash."

"That's the difference between fiction and real detective work, Caro – we first have to find the ash," Uncle Walter observed dryly.

The general layout of the solicitors' office appeared to be the same as the shop below - a large room immediately inside the entrance and a back room beyond. The front space had, however, been divided by a low partition wall that enabled a small reception room and a private office for Mr Skeene, whose name was sign written in gold block letters on the door. The back room door was equally annotated for Mr Roy.

Tobias went to that door, took a few steps forward and stopped, then a couple of side steps and stopped again.

"The ceiling panel in question should be right below me," he said, his voice soft and urgent.

He dropped to his knees and looked under the solicitor's desk a few feet away.

"There are soot marks on the underside, probably from a lamp," he said. He indicated the transom window high in the wall between the back and front rooms. "Where he was positioned, the desk acts as a shade so the light wouldn't be seen outside at night. And our friend was confident enough to leave it here over several days – there's an indent in the carpet."

Tobias looked down at the large Persian rug which covered much of the floor in the room. He went to the edge of the carpet and rolled it back until the floorboards were exposed.

Caro could see little in the dim office.

"We need more light," she said and Uncle Walter agreed, lighting the lamp on the desk and bringing it down to where Tobias now knelt, examining the floor. Caro drew closer to watch.

The two men discussed where to start before Uncle Walter pulled out his pen knife and inserted it between the butted ends of two of the boards. He levered up the end of one board by a fraction of an inch then, assisted by Tobias, pulled up the board. It seemed to come up easily.

"Jones!" called out Uncle Walter. The beadle rushed in. "Get downstairs to the jewellers; tell them they might have an expected visitor in the workroom shortly."

The man nodded, then vanished.

By then, Tobias had lifted the floorboards either side of the first, exposing the heavy cross cut joists supporting the floor and the ceiling below. "You can see what he's done here," he said. "He probably used a dovetail saw to cut flat on the back of the panel using the joists as a guide to the edges of the coffer. See how he's glued those blocks to use as handles?"

"Why bother with that?" asked Walter, frowning.

"So he could get it positioned just so when he was putting it back, I think."

"But he got it wrong by a fraction, didn't he?" said Caro. "That was the thin line of lighter coloured wood."

Tobias grinned up at her. "It was."

Walter reached down and lifted the panel out by the crude handles.

"Hello up there, sir!"

Jones the beadle, along with Hargreaves and his apprentice, peered up at them, then blinked as a small scattering of sawdust snowed gently down on them.

"So now we know how he got in," said Caro, stepping away from the hole in the floor, "but how did he get down and back up?"

Tobias rocked back on his haunches and stood up.

"Assuming it was just one man, he would have used a rope."

"But that would have to be tied to something..."

Uncle Walter looked up from studying the floor boards. "Look at this."

On the floorboards either side of the hole, at a right angle to the length of the removed boards, there were slight scuff marks.

"I'd say he turned one of the floorboards he pulled out to an angle across the opening and tied the rope round that."

Tobias quickly examined the boards they had removed. "I'd say you're right, Inspector," he said, indicating marks on one of them which seemed to be where the rope had been looped around it.

Walter pulled out his note pad. "This dratted man has kept my men occupied for the past month," he grumbled as he sketched out a diagram of the scene. "Heaven knows what he's doing with the gems he steals. We've visited every pawn broker and jewellery fence in every square inch of the city. Every police district in the country knows what to be on the lookout for but nothing has shown up. I can only think he's smuggling them abroad."

When the Inspector had finished his diagram and notes, Tobias replaced the cut out panel and began to put the floorboards back in place but suddenly stopped.

Caro watched him reach down in the void between the floor and the ceiling below a few feet to one side of the makeshift manhole.

"I've found something."

CHAPTER TEN

C aro caught a glimpse of gold. At first she thought it might have been a piece of jewellery, but as Tobias turned it, she saw it was nothing of the sort – though it was a 'ring' nonetheless.

"A cigar band," Uncle Walter observed.

"May I take a look?" Caro asked.

She held out her hand and Tobias's fingers lightly brushed hers as he laid the circle of paper in her palm. She turned it over. The artwork on it was exquisite. In an oval cartouche was an image of a pretty young woman. The colours were vivid red, blues and greens while the woman's skin colour was delicately rendered and her hair a honey blonde. She brushed a fingertip over the embossed scroll work covered in gold ink.

She had never closely examined a cigar band before but it seemed to her this one must be from a very expensive cigar, and she said so, handing it to Uncle Walter.

His manner was thoughtful as he turned the tiny circle of paper around in his hand.

"It looks near new. I don't think it's from when the arcade was built, and people collect cigar bands like these. You're right, my girl – this is from a very expensive cigar.

I'll have my men run down every tobacconist in the city; we might be able to find who sold the box this came in. It's another lead at least."

They put the solicitor's office to rights and locked it up once more. Caro slipped her arm through her uncle's as they walked along the balcony.

"Thank you for letting me accompany you today. I know mother doesn't approve, but it's just—"

"Shhh," he soothed, patting her arm. "You don't need to explain anything to me. Estelle just wants what's best for you. Besides, it's not all altruism on my part. You really do have a gift for detection and I'm not so proud as to refuse help."

Uncle Walter paused at the stop of the stairs. Caro looked at him questioningly.

"Just promise me one thing," he said.

"Of course."

"Don't go investigating on your own, will you, love?"

"I promise." Caro schooled her features into an innocent expression and waited for Tobias to call her on it. He didn't.

Soon they were out on the street. Uncle Walter hailed a hansom cab and directed the driver to take him to New Scotland Yard. Caro turned to Tobias and inclined her head.

"I suppose this is where we part company, Mr Black. Thank you for not saying anything to my uncle about our previous meeting. You have put me in your debt."

"You can repay the debt by calling me Tobias."

Caro smiled. "Then you must call me Caro, all my friends do."

"I'm glad to be included in their number," he answered. "Now, shall I call you a cab? Where are you heading?"

"Fitzrovia... I have to visit a friend."

Tobias nodded and looked out to the street. He raised a hand and whistled sharply. Up ahead, a top-hatted driver acknowledged the hail with a nod and negotiated the steady stream of traffic to reach the kerb. She gave the driver the address and found her hand in Tobias's as he aided her into the cab. He said something to the driver she missed, then, to her surprise, he climbed in after her and closed the cab doors with a slam.

"On, thank you, driver," he called and the carriage lurched into motion.

"I'll travel with you as far as Soho," he said, "there's someone I need to see."

There was something in Tobias's tone of voice that made her think the visit was not a professional one. A sweetheart perhaps? His wife?

She straightened her posture. Really, it was none of her business who he saw, just as her business was none of his. She thought of her upcoming interview with Bertie.

Oh Bertie, how can I refuse you and not ruin our friendship?

Caro remembered the scarf in her coat pocket.

"I have something of yours," she said, drawing the length of fabric out.

"Thank you. I was hoping you might find it," he replied, but made no move to take it from her.

The silence that suddenly came between them seemed awkward, almost oppressive in the intimate confines of the cab. Nothing at all like the easy familiarity of her friendship with Bertie.

"So…" she began, conscious of having his full attention. "How does a soldier become a magician?"

He smiled at her and she felt a tingling in her toes that became a warmth throughout her body. She no longer felt the outside cold.

"You have the question the wrong way about," he said. "It should have been how did a magician become a soldier."

"You've always been a magician?"

"In a way. My older brother taught me my first card trick when I was five. But when I grew up I knew I would have to make a proper living and I fancied to travel, so I chose the Army, went to Sandhurst and served in India, Yemen and Egypt.

"Then I had a run in with a girder."

"A Ghurka?"

"No," he smiled, "it really was a girder. An iron one. Very heavy. I was a lieutenant in the engineering corps stationed in Yemen. My company was sent out to build a bridge and to train some of the local men."

He shook his head at the recollection.

"I was climbing up some scaffolding to check on the work when a girder above, which hadn't been bolted securely, came down on top of me. I was pretty messed up." He touched a hand to his shoulder as if recalling.

"I broke a collar bone and my back was severely bruised from the fall.

"There was little I could do in my hospital bed while I recuperated, so my sergeant gave me a pack of playing cards. I got tired of Solitaire and, before I knew it, all those tricks I learned as a boy came back to me. I recovered and returned to England with my company five years ago. I thought I'd got the wanderlust out of me, but no sooner had I resigned my commission than I found myself hitching a ride across Germany with a troupe of itinerant performers. And found I was good at being a magician too.

"But now I'm home again, at my father's behest, and he's telling me once again I need to settle down, join my brother in business. So I shall. This will be the last season for The Dark Duke."

"Doesn't that make you sad?"

"Not really. In fact, I'm rather looking forward to it. I learned a lot as an engineer in the Army, so much that can be applied here at home – especially mechanical engineering. I think there's a time when one must 'put away childish things', don't you agree?"

She smiled at him but said nothing and turned to look out of the window. She thought of her law studies and her mother's opposing desire to see her daughter wed and with a family of her own. Perhaps it was time she grew up also, and take up her responsibilities. Perhaps it was selfish to hold onto her dream of becoming a lawyer.

She sighed inwardly.

Perhaps, despite her misgivings, she *should* accept Bertie's offer of marriage. After all, who knew her better than he did? At least he would let her finish her studies and not demand she break them off immediately.

She was unaware she was lost in her own thoughts until she sensed Tobias watching her closely. She turned to face him and felt a heated blush burn her cheeks. There was something in his expression which fascinated her and, for a moment, she felt a deep longing. What would it be like to kiss him?

"Now there's a trick – disappearing so far into your own thoughts you were no longer here," he said, his voice barely audible over the steady clip-clop of the horse and the sound of the traffic around them. "A penny for them?"

She inclined her head, as much to distract herself from the question she had just posed herself, as it was to answer his enquiry, she spoke.

"You were talking about the future, making the decision to grow up and move on. I was just thinking about *my* future. There's a decision I've been putting off making... partly because the dream I have to be a lawyer is really just a fantasy, and partly because there is something comfortable in holding onto one's dreams – even the unattainable ones."

She paused and frowned before continuing.

"You're lucky. You've pursued your passions, not once but twice. The thought of simply being someone's wife with no identity of my own..." She shook her head. "I'm sorry. I shouldn't be talking like this."

"I'm glad you feel you can," he said. "This decision you're making... is that part of your errand today?"

She nodded. A lump had formed in her throat. She felt the cab slow and approach the kerb.

"Soho, Sir."

Tobias acknowledged the driver, then took Caro's hands in his.

"My father gave me a word of advice in his last letter, the one which prompted me to come home – 'don't follow your passion, but always bring it with you'. Life and circumstance doesn't always give us what we want, but there is always something better if you're willing to look for it."

He opened the door and she started to pull her hands away, but Tobias kept hold of one and dropped a brief kiss on the back of it.

"Until we meet again... Caro."

The cab pulled away and she swallowed the lead in her throat as she watched familiar streets pass by, bringing her closer to her decision, closer to her fate, her destiny.

CHAPTER ELEVEN

An understanding Bertie shrugged off her apology for missing their previous day's appointment. Then a look of surprise crossed his face as she explained the reason why she wasn't at home when he called.

She told him everything – the interview with Tobias Black at the Palladian Theatre and all that transpired afterwards, including the discovery of the trap door into the jewellery store and the discovery of the expensive cigar band.

"Well, The Phantom might be a thief but at least he took the band off before smoking his cigar, not like those uncouth blighters at the Gilfroys' party."

"What do you mean?" Caro asked

"The acrobats who performed. I was on the terrace and I saw them in the garden smoking a cigar. I only remember it because I thought how unmannerly it was to leave the band on. What did the one Mr Black find look like?"

As she described it to him, Bertie's mouth fell open.

"I say – that sounds like the same type the acrobat had."

"You were close enough to see it?"

Bertie blushed. "Well, no. Not while he was smoking it. Oh, how embarrassing, Caro. I know it sounds terribly grubby but when the chap threw it away and went back inside, I..." He hesitated and his face flushed even deeper. "I went and picked it up."

"Why?"

"I know it sounds juvenile and I hope you'll forgive me, but I collect cigar bands and I just couldn't help seeing if it wasn't one I already had..."

Caroline smiled. *Dear Bertie*. "Was it?"

"No. And it was an expensive one too. I thought it was odd some circus performer type was smoking expensive cigars. And he'd thrown half of it away."

He paused a moment as if in thought, then his face lit up.

"Same cigars and both at robberies by The Phantom! You don't think the acrobats are his henchmen, do you?"

Caro recalled the damage at the scene of the Gilfroy's robbery and its contrast with The Phantom's crimes.

"Uncle Walter doesn't think Sir Hubert was robbed by The Phantom and neither do I. But we should tell him about the acrobats and the cigar. Come on, where do you keep your notepaper?"

Bertie rose to do her bidding. She dictated the note to him and he blotted it and folded it.

"The chap who marries you, Caro," he commented lightly as he sealed the envelope, "isn't going to have a minute's peace."

Caro licked her lips. She recalled her conversation with Tobias.

"You said there was something you wanted to ask me, the reason why you came by yesterday?"

She was proud of the way she spoke the sentence without her voice breaking. She had decided. When he asked her to marry him, she would accept. It would make him happy and it would certainly make her mother happy. Overjoyed, in fact. And, just as Tobias said, whatever the future brought, she would take her passion along with her.

And yet Bertie was apparently oblivious to her nervousness. He shook his head and tapped the envelope.

"It can wait. Let's get this message to your uncle. I can't wait to tell Eddie about this. Your uncle will have to let us in on it now – this is going to be the most exciting Christmas ever!"

All of a sudden Caro's mood lifted and she felt the same giddy excitement she experienced as a little girl at the age of ten when, one summer at Bertie's family estate, her older brother and his best friend decided she wasn't too young to go rambling with them.

She remembered that season well. They had walked for miles and miles through fields, played war games on the banks of the stream with the local children whose parents worked on the estate. They picnicked under a grove of apple trees and only went back to the house at twilight.

Perhaps married life could be like that for them. Full of carefree companionship – Edward and Gwen, her and Bertie... Perhaps it would work out just fine after all.

Bertie interrupted her thoughts.

"Let's drop the note off at Scotland Yard ourselves. And do you mind if we stop off at the Arcade on the way there? I need your feminine opinion on something," he asked.

"No, of course I don't mind," she replied.

* * *

Caro's butterflies returned as Bertie led her into the jeweller's.

"Miss Caroline! A pleasure to see you again," said the jeweller. "I hope you've come to tell me that you've single-handedly apprehended The Phantom."

"Alas not, Mr Hargreaves," she answered, "that is most certainly a job best left for the police. I'm here on a professional matter – your profession."

Bertie looked up from the glass case in front of him.

"May I see the rings in that tray please?"

Mr Hargreaves was only too happy to oblige.

Bertie fingered row upon row of rings before pulling out two. The first was an oval cut sapphire – from Ceylon, the jeweller informed them – surrounded with round diamonds and mounted in gold. The second gold ring featured a faceted stone that shone pinks, blues and greens – Alexandrite, Caro learned – and that stone was surrounded by tiny seed pearls.

Bertie held them both out to Caro.

"You're really good at hypotheticals, Caro, so let me try this one on you. If you were going to be surprised with a ring, which one would you prefer?"

Caro quelled her nerves and gave the question serious thought before answering.

"Both rings are absolutely beautiful, but I don't think it would be much of a surprise if the girl knew she was getting a choice!"

Bertie shook his head with a smile and swept away the fringe that flopped over his brow.

"Seriously? You're not going to tell me which one I ought to get?"

"I'm not the one proposing – you're going to have to do that for yourself." Caro grew serious. "But, this being a purely hypothetical question, let me put it back onto you. When you think of the girl you are planning to surprise, which ring reminds you of her?"

Bertie looked thoughtful for a moment and turned back to Mr Hargreaves.

"Could you put these two rings aside for me for the next few days, while I think about it?"

* * *

O come, all ye faithful, joyful and triumphant!
O come ye, O come ye to Bethlehem;
Come and behold him
Born the King of Angels:
O come, let us adore Him
O come, let us adore Him
O come, let us adore Him
Christ the Lord

The harmonies of the choir in their white and red costumes rose above the din in the foyer of the grandest and newest hotel in London, the Longmuir.

Caro was the first to arrive and she positioned herself on a sofa with a newspaper in hand, only half reading the stories inside. The front page of the broadsheet made her very nervous indeed.

PHANTOM WOES GROW!
MPs call for resignations at the Yard
Fears for famed Star of December Diamond

Adding to her unease was a rather greasy and unprepossessing man who had been loitering around the hotel reception. He looked impatient and didn't really care whether he drew attention to himself or not. His clothes were well enough made but they were crumpled, as though he had slept in them.

She caught him looking at her more than once, but she made sure they never made eye contact.

"Caro, sweetheart!"

Her head shot up at the sound of her name, especially followed by the endearment. And she was surprised further to see the man who had called out was Tobias, now moving towards her, past the oily looking man.

"Business took a little longer than I thought," he continued in the same light, slightly over loud tone. Caro stood, almost in surprise more than anything else. Tobias removed the paper from her hand and dropped it on the sofa. His lips moved towards her cheek as though he might kiss it, but instead he whispered: "That man is a reporter for one of the tabloid rags. He's after your uncle. We're to wait for him in Count Valois's apartments."

Caro was still taking in his words when the effect of his breath on her ear sent shivers down her back that had nothing to do with the chill outside.

His hand was at her elbow. He urged her past the reporter who, Caro noticed, had ceased to pay any attention to her now it seemed she had a beau. They moved further into the foyer. Set between the grand curved staircases which rose to the first floor ballroom was a black iron cage that extended straight up, disappearing into the void above.

Tall doors set with glass opened at ground level as they approached, then the brass lattice scissor gate in front of the doors drew open and a page, not much older than twelve years but looking resplendent in his uniform of a red jacket with bright brass buttons and black trousers, stepped aside and let his passengers disembark.

Caro had read about this in the papers – the Longmuir's passenger lift was an absolute sensation when it opened five years ago – but she had not yet seen it for herself.

She allowed Tobias to lead her into the claustrophobic oak-lined box.

"I saw a few more of those reporters hanging around the lobby," he said softly. "We need to do a disappearing trick of our own before they recognise me."

They were joined in the lift by an elderly couple. The man was tall and lean, not stooped as his age might indicate. His wife was half his height but twice as wide, although that may have had as much to do with her large sable fur coat as her natural size.

As the page squeezed back in and closed the doors, Caro found herself pressed against Tobias in the confined space – and did not find it at all unpleasant.

"Floor seven," said the elderly man with a seeming air of pride in his voice at nominating the next-to-top floor.

"The Royal Suite please," said Tobias.

"Floor eight? Yes, sir," replied the page.

Caro saw the elderly man's wife eye them with a mixture of awe and envy.

The boy closed the scissor gate, then the glass door before engaging the telemotor that controlled the lift. The box jerked upward with a little lurch. Tobias surreptitiously took her hand as if he already knew it was Caro's first time in an elevator. She had to admit to herself that the experience of travelling through floors was a little disconcerting.

Following a stop on the seventh floor for the elderly couple to get out, finally they arrived at the upper most floor of the hotel where there were only three apartments. The largest, the Royal Suite, was occupied by Count Valois.

They were greeted in the hallway by the Count's equerry, a smartly turned out middle-aged man with greying hair.

Before the man could speak, Tobias presented him with a card.

"Captain Tobias Black at your service and this is Miss Caroline Addison," he said. The equerry responded with a short bow. "I apologise for our unannounced entrance," Tobias continued, "but there are reporters gathering by the score for the arrival of Detective Chief Inspector Addison. I thought it wise to remain inconspicuous and come up ahead."

"A wise move, Captain Black. Please to accompany me to the sitting room where you may await the Inspector's arrival. I shall let the Count know you are here."

Caroline's eyes widened at the splendour of the sitting room. It was larger than the parlour at home and sumptuously decorated in cream and gold brocade fabric wallpaper. A fire burned in the hearth although it barely seemed necessary – the room itself seemed to exude warmth.

She gravitated towards the window, drawing back a sheer lace curtain to look out over the extended sill down onto the busy London junction below and the misty park beyond. It was an impressive view from this height, though the day, which had begun with such promise had, by this afternoon, started to cloud over again, and the world below was cast in a pall.

The large windows were shut against the cold. She imagined that in summer they would be thrown open to let in air.

She dropped the curtain and turned to see Tobias stalking the room like a caged panther. He stopped when he saw he was being watched. She smiled.

"I don't pretend to be a mind reader, but I can guess what *you're* doing."

Tobias lifted his chin, silently inviting elucidation.

"You're looking to see how he might do it – the Phantom, that is."

"Studying the lay of the land is something the Army taught me."

"Well, unless he can scale walls, I can't see him getting in through these windows."

"Some people could…"

"What do you mean?"

Before he could reply, the equerry re-entered the room with Uncle Walter and announced Count Valois would be with them momentarily.

Tobias leaned in and spoke softly. "I think a bigger trick than getting through that window is going to be convincing the Count to go along with your uncle's plan."

CHAPTER TWELVE

"It is the proposal *fantastique, monsieur l'inspector!*"
Count Maurice Valois was a roly-poly little man
nearly half a head shorter than Caro herself.
She found herself staring at the pronounced widow's
peak of his black hair, made even more alarming by the
way it was slicked back.

The Count may have been informally dressed in a grey
day suit, but the wide red sash across his white shirt and
a gold and enamel star hanging from it like a pendant
made Caro feel decidedly poorly attired in comparison.

"Scotland Yard's fame, it is known all over the
continent, but never before have I known officers of the
law employ charming young ladies in the pursuit of the
criminal classes," he proclaimed.

Caro accepted the compliment with a polite dip of her
head but was pleased when her uncle spoke and drew the
strange little man's attention away from her.

"We believe we now know the identity of the man
behind the thefts of diamond jewellery throughout
London over the past two months," said Uncle Walter,
eliciting a soft gasp of surprise from Caro.

When did that happen?

"We've learned that the first of these thefts occurred within two days of the arrival of Rudolph Van Dyke."

"*Him?* Bah!" exclaimed the count, throwing his hands in the air. "That man has coveted my diamond for many, many years and now you say he will resort to stealing it from me? Why don't you arrest him?"

"We have no evidence we can charge him with. However, we also know now that he is not working alone. He has two accomplices – a pair of circus acrobats."

This time, Caro's mouth fell open. "What?"

It was Tobias who provided the answer.

"Remember the other day when I travelled with you as far as Soho? We may have gone our separate ways but we ended up on the same track. While you were putting two and two together with your friend Bertie, I was checking with a friend of mine who is in touch with the immigrant communities in London. Van Dyke was a commanding officer in the Prussian Army and his subordinates included Pavel – one of the acrobats from the show. So well done connecting the clues of the cigar bands."

"Thieves and scoundrels!" exclaimed the Count. "Such men should be – how is it you say in your country – 'locked up and the key thrown away'?"

"You may be right, Count," said Caro, "but in this country we have *jurisprudence*. We can't arrest anyone on suspicion without very strong grounds. And as my uncle says, we have no evidence to satisfy a judge."

"Which brings us here today to go into the details of our plan to protect the Star of December diamond," Walter concluded. "May we see where you keep the gem?"

"But of course. Please to follow me."

With precise, almost mincing steps, the Count led them down the passageway of his suite to the decadently appointed bedroom and straight to a cabinet. He opened the rosewood doors. Behind it was a safe.

"I had the combination reset to my own design and only *I* know it," he said as his surprisingly long and delicate fingers fingered the combination dial this way and that until they heard the click of the lock opening.

"I suppose you will want to see the Star of December for yourself," he said and looking at Caro specifically. "I imagine a young lady will be most fascinated."

The Count opened the safe door and withdrew an ebony box, unadorned but for the brass escutcheon, and carried it to a nearby table. He pulled out a watch chain on which was attached a little key, opened the case with a theatrical flourish and took out a cover of black velvet. There, sitting inside the fitted case, was the most brilliant stone Caro had ever seen. It was as blue as the sky and it glittered in the well lit room.

"It's magnificent," she breathed.

"You think so? I have a surprise for you. This is *not* the Star of December."

"No?"

"*Non.* Allow me to explain."

The Count lifted out the deep velvet tray in which the apparent gem sat. Beneath seemed at first glance to be the plain ebony bottom of the box, but now the Count produced a slender gold toothpick and inserted it in what was little more than a pin hole in the inside back plate of the box's main half-mortise lock. With a soft click, the inside bottom of the box popped up at one edge, revealing a hidden compartment below. The Count removed it to reveal a shallow fitted compartment containing another stone, exactly like the first.

"*This* is the real Star of December. The other is a decoy only, made of glass."

"Bravo, Count, an ingenious hidden compartment," said Tobias who approached. "May I?" He examined it closely for a moment.

The Count smiled at Caro. "Perhaps Miss Addison would like to hold the jewel that once adorned an emperor's sceptre, and a queen's crown? The Star of December has a history that goes back to when another queen, Queen Elizabeth, sat on England's throne."

He picked the diamond out of its recess and placed it on the palm of her hand. By her estimation it measured one inch in diameter and a quarter of an inch deep. Although it weighed comparatively little, she was conscious of it sitting on her palm. Its facets glinted and sparkled as she moved it around her hand and when she looked at the face of it again, the points of the star became more pronounced.

"It is truly magnificent, Count," she breathed, unable to take her eyes off it. No wonder this man Van Dyke coveted it for himself. Even the beautiful, brilliant white diamond butterfly brooch taken from the Barrington Arcade could not compare with this singularly magnificent gem.

Reluctantly, she handed back the stone. Valois lovingly fitted the treasure into its secret compartment, then closed and locked the box, which then went back into the safe.

And with a turn of the handle and a spin of the dial, the safe was sealed.

"Now you have seen my little treasure and the length I go to protect it, I would like to hear, dear Inspector, your plans in detail to keep it safe during the exhibition here at the hotel."

CHAPTER THIRTEEN

C aro put a hand flat to her stomach and looked at her reflection in the mirror.

Her gown was the colour of her favourite caramel fudge. The soft pleated satin of the neckline was gathered at the shoulders which were decorated with feathers of tan and black. The bodice was covered in matching hail spot tulle. The line of the gown was nipped in at the waist and fell to just above her ankles. The skirt shimmered as she walked.

It was a magnificent gown, designed by a professional costumier selected by Tobias and fitted just for her, with Count Valois footing the bill. She winced a little at the cost, especially considering not one but two gowns had been made – and one of them would never be worn.

Spectacular though it was, the gown was something she would never have chosen for herself, but Tobias had explained to everyone that for the performance to work, every eye - men's and women's alike – needed to be focused on her.

"It's Caro who will be the real star of the show," he had told them. "My job is to be unobtrusive until just the right moment."

And for the rest of the week she and Tobias rehearsed several hours a day in a salon at the lavish Richmond home of the Count's friend, the Duke of Teck. Each night on her return home, Caro collapsed into bed to sleep dreamlessly until one of the maids woke her at seven in the morning to start all over again.

The reflection that stared back at her was nearly a stranger. Her eyelids were smudged with something resembling soot and a coloured pencil was drawn across her brows, making them stand out against her naturally fair skin. Her lips were stained the colour of berries.

She used a lot more make up than she would normally wear but she was assured by Georgette, the theatre choreographer whom Tobias had hired, that all of this paint was necessary to stand out as a performer.

From out in the salon she could hear the chamber orchestra start to play.

"Are you ready, *ma cherie?*" Georgette asked. "Just a few minutes now."

Caro nodded and stood, feeling the fabric of her gown fall. She ran a long scarf of matching satin through her hands. From behind the screen she watched the assembly of more than a hundred invited guests file through the doors into the large room.

The chamber orchestra was seated in a corner of the room and in the middle of the space stood a plinth about three feet high draped with a black cloth that fell to the floor all around it. Atop the plinth stood a display box with bevelled glass panels on all four sides and an ostentatiously large padlock in glittering silver securing the door.

The milling people approached the plinth and Caro heard their murmurs of disappointment as they spied an empty display case. They had all come to see the Star of December but all that was inside was a vacant velvet-lined mount. They weren't to know it, but there was a surprise waiting.

Caro leaned out as far as she dared to see if there were faces she recognised.

Her brother and Bertie were somewhere about, given charge by Uncle Walter to keep an eye out for suspicious characters in the crowd.

There was her mother and father with Uncle Walter. Gwen and Margaret walked in arm in arm, Gwen in cobalt blue that set off her pale skin and black hair, Margaret in raspberry red that brought colour to her cheeks and highlights to her blonde hair.

Uncle Walter had said some of his best men would be in the room but dressed in tails, and she was hard pressed to pick any of them. And waiting for her in another room off the hotel salon was Tobias, getting ready for the performance.

To help quell her nervousness, Caro softly hummed along to the tune the orchestra played.

The music came to an end and other piece began. After this, Count Valois would emerge.

She smiled, recalling how she had thoroughly enjoyed spending the past few days with Tobias at their rehearsal studio at White Lodge. Any concerns her parents and brother might have had about them spending so much time together, was assuaged by Uncle Walter vouching for Tobias.

Her new friend was an excellent tutor and they talked and laughed as much as they rehearsed. Again and again, the polyphon was wound up in the salon and the tune played until in the end she got the performance down perfectly. It was remarkable how well they seemed to work together in such a short space of time.

With the help of Mademoiselle Georgette, they had perfected a routine for this one night only.

Caro closed her eyes, recalling their final rehearsal only a few hours previously. Even now she could feel the touch of Tobias's hand as he held her in their dance. Perhaps it was because of the romantic story Georgette had devised for them – a fairytale performance that would result in the Star of December magically appearing in the case – that her heart beat a little faster.

The orchestra ended with a flourish and the hubbub of voices quietened.

From her vantage point, she saw the Count's equerry step out in front of the orchestra and call the attention of the guests before asking them to please gather around the perimeter of the room. A few moments later, Count Valois entered, crisply turned out in black evening dress with a sash of vivid red satin across his chest. And that chest was filled with medals which Tobias quipped might have been bought from a curiosity shop on the high street.

"*Monsieurs et Mesdames*, ladies and gentlemen, thank you," he said, standing before the orchestra, his voice much louder than his size would suggest. "Tonight, to help reveal such a precious gem as The Star of December, we have a special presentation for you.

"The Star of December is unsurpassed in its magnificence. It has been coveted by kings, desired by the most beautiful of women. My humble self cannot express in words its value – not in monetary terms, *non, non, non,* that is but of secondary importance to the *romance* of this stone.

"*Alors*, rather than tell you, I shall show you in the story of The Thief of Hearts. Orchestra, if you please."

The musicians began to play a dramatic intermezzo that would bridge to the performance.

"It is time, *cherie*," Georgette prompted and Caro turned back into the side room where, lid yawning open, the lacquered Egyptian-styled chest on its low stand with handles like a sedan chair awaited her.

Georgette helped her step into the chest and arranged her gown so she could crouch down and get into position on her side.

"Ready?"

"Yes," she replied and closed her eyes to steady her nerves. She felt the space become claustrophobically close, heard a rustling sound as the second gown was placed in the chest and, a moment later, the firm clunk of the lid closing.

"Come in now," Georgette called out, beckoning the two men who would carry the chest into the salon atop the special stand that Caro had learned was referred to as a deceptive table.

From inside in darkness, she could only imagine the scene unfolding as she felt the chest being lifted by the men, and smiled at Tobias's cheek at suggesting two uniformed constables carry the chest into the room – and her uncle's sense of humour in agreeing to arrange it.

The chest and stand rocked gently as it was carried into the salon to the applause of the gathering. Caro knew from rehearsals the box would be placed gently down several feet to one side of the plinth and display case.

The gasp she then heard from the audience must, she supposed, be their reaction to Tobias's entry from the other side of the room. She knew he would cross quickly to her and the performance would begin.

"Ladies and gentlemen," she heard him say as the orchestra quieted on cue, "permit me if you please to introduce myself. I am The Dark Duke."

The audience applauded politely and a voice called out that Caro recognised. It was Bertie.

"I say, have you got the Star of December in there?"

"I am sorry to disappoint you," replied Tobias above a smattering of laughter, "but this chest is as empty as *that* display case."

Caro heard the chest lid being opened and Tobias went into the act, lifting out and holding up to audience the second gown. "The only thing in here is this dress and nothing more."

He invited one of the ladies to approach and look into the chest to confirm it was vacant. Caro knew the woman looking in would see nothing but an empty box lined with striped fabric but couldn't help but hold her breath until she heard her confirm it.

"And the dress? That is unoccupied also?" asked Tobias, a smile in his voice, and the woman laughed and confirmed that too.

"Then let's just put it back in the chest," said Tobias and a moment later the lid closed with a clunk once more and the orchestra took up the first notes of Brahms's Ballade in D-minor, not only setting the tone for the rest of the performance – dark, mysterious, intriguing – but also covering any noise Caro might make within the chest. She stiffened, ready to move.

"Alas!" Tobias called out loudly, giving Caro her cue. As he continued to address the audience, she sprang into action, opening the hinged half panel of the false floor and drawing the second gown down into the deceptive table below. Moving quickly but with care not to trap her own gown, she moved atop the fixed portion of the chest floor and closed the hatch. After several dozen rehearsals in the last few days, she achieved it all in just the time it took Tobias to speak.

"An empty display cabinet and a dress within an empty chest!" proclaimed Tobias. "Such a puzzle, ladies and gentlemen! Where could the Star of December be?"

At that, he raised the chest lid and Caro stood. The audience gasped and applauded as Tobias held out his hand to help her step out of the chest.

With a flourish, he passed his hand beside her head and the spectacular blue gem was suddenly in his grasp as if he had plucked it from her ear. He held it up to another gasp from the surrounding crowd as Caro raised her satin scarf and turned in a circle, trailing the fabric with arm held high.

Caro began to dance. With the eyes of the audience on her, it allowed Tobias to slip away with the two hotel footmen who swiftly carried away the chest and stand.

Mademoiselle Georgette had told her to feel the music and it would guide her steps. The choreographer was right. Suddenly, it was as if there was no audience. It was just Caro and the music.

The scarf in her hand moved as she moved, either trailing behind her or fluttering above her head when she held it aloft. She moved around the plinth and empty cabinet and the surrounding crowd fell back a little further from it. She fully understood the importance of the scarf in the upcoming misdirection. Her job was to make sure everyone noticed it and saw it as part of her.

She danced alone for almost a minute, then the music changed, becoming darker and more dramatic. At that point, Tobias re-emerged into the circle around the plinth, half his face covered by a white satin mask making a dramatic counterpoint to his black top hat and evening dress complete with cape lined in red satin.

He wove his way towards Caro, playing his part of a mysterious villain tempting the maiden ever closer with the beautiful blue stone in his hand. How the guests gasped yet again when he opened his hand and held it aloft. Caro caught it flashing in the light and smiled to herself. The audience was not to know it was the glass replica.

She and Tobias skirted one another around the empty display case. Chase, retreat, entice, break free – all in time to the music and circling closer and closer to the plinth. Then, at last, the maiden was caught – lured by The Thief of Hearts and the magic in the stone.

In character, Caro did her best to resist, putting the plinth and cabinet between herself and the Thief. Tobias stretched his hands as though offering the stone. Caro leaned towards him as though hypnotised.

He stepped around and approached, his hands moving in the air. Hers followed suit, the scarf in her hand fluttered above her. Then he captured one end of the scarf and used it to draw her closer. Finally, the maiden was unable to resist, taking the stone in her hand and holding it up, always keeping it in view of the audience.

Tobias turned in a tight circle, his cape flaring out, then snatched away both the stone and the scarf.

In an instant, he flared the satin over his hand and appeared to press the sparkling gem into it, rolling and turning and bundling the Star of December into the ball of shimmering fabric, turning full circle as he did so to show the action to the crowd.

When, in the very next moment, he flicked the satin out across the padlocked display cabinet like a maid throwing a sheet open across a bed and the fabric fell, draping the glass-sided box, a shocked sharp intake of breath came from the crowd.

What had happened to the Star of December?

The answer came in the next second as Tobias whisked away the satin scarf and the diamond was revealed magically transported inside the locked display cabinet, sitting majestically in the previously empty velvet mount.

A general gasp of surprise rose up. "It's there!" said a breathless woman.

Success!

The *ballade* closed and the room burst into cheers and applause. Tobias bowed and turned. He picked up Caro's hand and bowed over it before bringing her forward to join him in accepting the ovation. Caro bowed as he had done.

"You were superb!" he whispered before taking another bow.

CHAPTER FOURTEEN

aro's cheeks ached. She couldn't recall a time when she had ever smiled so much. She accepted congratulations from guests and again from her family, but still, she was glad for the respite when, after an hour of circulating among the guests as they admired the Star of December on display in the glass case, the guests filed away from the salon towards the dining room for supper.

Tobias too had no shortage of admirers – particularly of the female kind, she noted with a smile. Still, it was strange that whenever she looked for him in the crowd, his eyes always seemed to find hers.

When the guests had left the room, she and Tobias waited with Uncle Walter at the display cabinet and the Count returned with the ebony box.

"Ah, *merveilleux*, the show was a tremendous success, was it not?" said the Count. "Such a performance! It will make all the newspapers and many people will come to see the Star of December for the full day showing tomorrow."

"And now, before I join you for the supper *mes amis*, I shall put my beauties to bed."

Tobias unlocked the cabinet door and took the diamond from within, and produced the replica from his waistcoat pocket. The Count took them one at a time and restored them to their respective compartments in the ebony box.

Just as he and Walter moved off, Tobias interjected.

"Do you mind if I accompany you and the Inspector to your suite?" he asked.

"But of course!" the Count agreed heartily. "I shall feel especially well guarded in the company of no less prominent personages than a Detective Chief Inspector of Scotland Yard and The Dark Duke, the cleverest magician in all of England. I did want to talk to you about your phenomenal trick tonight. You will tell me how it was done, yes?"

Before Tobias answered, Walter chimed in, giving a smile to the small group.

"I think you'll find, Count Valois, that magicians – like detectives – are bound to secrecy."

* * *

After dinner, a select group accepted the Baron's invitation to end the evening with sherry in his apartments. They rode up the eight floors in the lift and when they emerged on the top floor, a uniformed officer greeted them.

"Been all quiet here, sir," he told the Inspector, "No one has been through who hasn't been a verified guest or staff." He lifted up a clipboard as evidence of his diligence.

Another uniformed officer stood at the entrance to the Count's suites. He too had nothing of interest to report.

No one had lingered and no one went past him along the corridor either.

"Well, it looks like we're safe then," said Walter. "Get Davies and head off duty, you've earned a break."

"Thank you, sir," the young man said with something that sounded like relief.

The equerry moved past them and hastened to light more lamps and prepare drinks while the Baron excused himself to go to his private rooms.

"It seems like all of this preparation was an anti-climax," said Edward as he took two drinks from the proffered tray and handed one to Gwen who was seated on the leather chair by the fire. "Perhaps we were wrong, perhaps The Phantom or Van Dyke, whatever this character's name is, isn't really interested in the Star of December diamond at all."

"You're as bad as your sister," smiled Bertie. "Detective work is methodical, detailed and slow. Tonight's performance might have frightened off the thieves. They might decide to strike at another time in another city."

"Well, we can but hope he and his gang have been so completely frightened off by the esteemed detectives of Scotland Yard that they would never dream of committing such a theft," Margaret added.

Tobias raised a glass.

"A toast – to Scotland Yard and her hardworking detectives!"

Everyone raised a glass.

After the toast, Caroline's mother found the piano and started playing softly.

Tobias approached Caro and bowed to her.

"Would you care to dance?"

She accepted his hand and rose to her feet.

"You were absolutely perfect tonight," he said. "I can't tell you how enjoyable this week has been for me."

Despite herself, Caro blushed. "Me too," she replied and they danced in silence for a minute. He seemed quite contented but her mind roiled. "What are you doing for Christmas?" she asked at last.

"I'm catching the train to Lancashire in the next couple of days to spend it with my family."

"Oh..." was all she could say.

As they danced, Caro caught Margaret's eye. Her friend raised an eyebrow, asking a question she was too polite to broach tonight. Tomorrow, however, there would be an interrogation more thorough than any detective's.

Caro was attracted to Tobias, of that there was little doubt anymore, but to be honest, the thought of something more than an acquaintance borne of this adventure hadn't fully occurred to her. But now it took root as they danced. It had blossomed into something more for him too; she could see it in his eyes. And yet, after tonight, she wouldn't see him again.

Bertie tapped Tobias on the shoulder.

"May I cut in?"

Tobias bowed and backed away, letting Bertie take her hand. Caro's disappointment, though kept to herself, was nearly smothering.

"You're probably tired of hearing it, but you were wonderful tonight, Caro, just terrific," he said. She smiled tiredly at his enthusiasm. Then he turned serious. "I really *have* to see you tomorrow. Will you promise you'll be at home? Promise me you'll be there. It's important to me. *Very* important. You won't let me down, will you?"

A lump formed in her throat, and she was surprised at the strength of her emotion.

"I won't, Bertie, I promise. Come early to our Christmas Eve party and–"

A scream rent the air. Count Valois rushed into the sitting room, his face ghostly pale.

"*Mon dieu, mon dieu,* I cannot believe it! The Star of December is *gone!*"

CHAPTER FIFTEEN

Tobias reacted before anyone and ran into the Count's suite. Uncle Walter followed quickly behind. Caro pushed her way into the room and saw the safe open. The ebony box too was open... and empty.

"But how?" The Count's voice trailed away to a whisper.

"Concentrate, it's very important, Count. You put the diamond in the safe after the exhibition when everyone went to dinner, correct?" asked Walter.

"I did," he answered. "You were there, along with Monsieur Black. He was most interested in which was the glass decoy and which was the real diamond."

"That's right," Tobias confirmed.

The distraught Valois continued. "I thought I heard a sound just a minute ago and I came in here but there was nothing amiss. I opened the safe and the box - then *poof!* The Star of December is disappeared!"

Caro sensed something, felt it before she saw it. Saw *him*.

She turned and looked directly at the window. Outside – eight floors above the ground – a man looked in, almost masked by the silk lace curtain. "There's a man outside!"

Tobias was closest. He tore away the curtain and flung open the window but the man was gone. Tobias looked out. "He's making his way along the ledge!"

Before anyone could react, he had climbed out the window after him. Edward and Bertie, along with the equerry, started to follow.

Walter barked at them. "Don't be fools, you three, you wouldn't stand a chance! Come with me. He'll have to come back in through one of the other suites – we'll get him even if we have to break through every door. James!" Caro's father stood to attention. "Find a bobby and get someone up here now!"

Soon – with the exception of Count Valois, who had slumped into a chair – only the women remained. Caro rushed to the window and leaned out. Her panting breath plumed in the freezing winter air and was whisked away by the stiff breeze.

To her left, she saw Tobias and the other man, a skulking figure in black, against the midnight blue sky. Looking down, she was stricken with vertigo and looked back across at Tobias in alarm. One misstep and he could plummet to his death!

"Come away from the window, Caroline," her mother advised.

"I can't," she said.

Suddenly she felt warmth. Gwen and Margaret huddled close behind her. Dear Margaret had drawn a shawl over her shoulders.

Together, they watched the nimble thief sidle along the ledge, his experience as an acrobat evident in the confident advance. Tobias was three yards behind, gamely moving forward, but noticeably less surefooted.

Wind hit the building broadside. Tobias braced himself and waited for the gust to ebb away but it seemed not to bother the thief at all. Now he was at least five yards ahead and rapidly approaching the corner of the building. Once around it, he might be gone for good.

Still, Tobias moved valiantly on.

Further ahead, she caught movement. Someone had opened a window and was beckoning the thief!

She leaned out to count just how many windows along before she was pulled back in by Gwen and Margaret.

"Quick! We have to tell Uncle Walter," Caro said, bustling past her mother and a rather surprised Count Valois. "Eight windows along, he'll be in there. Come on!"

She ran down the passage with the rest of their party following behind. Bertie and Edward were taking it in turns to shoulder charge a door. A moment later, the door gave in and the two men barrelled through followed by Walter.

Loud thumps and the sound of glass breaking attested to the struggle going on inside. Caro hesitated at the door, unsure whether to follow into the melee. It was all but over when she entered the room. Bertie and Edward held one man by the arms, the fight apparently gone out of him. Tobias and Walter had cornered the other, but it seemed he was not going to make it an easy arrest.

The big window in the room was wide open behind him, letting out the heat from the fire which burned brightly in the hearth.

"Give it up, Pavel. It's too late for you and Nemec," Tobias panted heavily. "You can't escape now."

Walter stepped forward. "Hand it over, Pavel."

As Caro would later recall it, everything seemed to happen in slow motion.

The man named Pavel glanced at his friend and then back to Walter. He pulled out the blue diamond from his pocket and held it up to the light where it scintillated. Then he lobbed it into the air.

Tobias and Walter tackled Pavel to the ground. Nemec struggled free of Bertie and Edward and surged forward, reaching out for the stone with both arms. Edward grabbed Nemec again by one arm and Bertie, flailing, struck the other. Nemec's fingertips gave the stone a glancing tap, making it leap and pirouette into the air once more.

Caro, and indeed everyone, saw the Star of December flash like lightning as it tumbled over and over in mid-air until it fell onto the grate.

And shatter into a thousand little pieces.

* * *

Gwen screamed. The Count fainted. Caro gasped as one large diamond became hundreds of little sparkling splinters lit by the tongues of fire. When she turned to Walter and Tobias, there were twin expressions of shock on both their faces as they looked back from the open window, the curtain billowing in the wind from outside.

And Pavel was nowhere to be seen.

"Great Scott! What happened here?"

Caro turned to the voice. It was her father. Behind him stood two bobbies on alert.

Walter pointed to Nemec. "Take this one away. The other one... good Lord. I can't believe he did that!"

"Did what?" asked Caro's father.

"He somersaulted backwards out of the window."

"Eight floors up? Then surely–"

"–Not so fast, Mr Addison," said Tobias who turned to lean out of the window once more. Over the wind Caro heard a faint cry of pain.

"There's a balconette one floor below this. He's broken an ankle by the looks of it."

Nemec apparently saw the wisdom of going peacefully and allowed himself to be handcuffed between the two police officers.

"Take him down to the station first," said Uncle Walter. "We'll go downstairs and let Mr Pavel ponder the wisdom of his actions for a little while longer."

Caroline looked at poor Count Valois, now recovering on the couch. He looked as if his entire world had come to an end. What a dreadful thing to have happen to such a beautiful stone, and yet...

"Diamonds don't shatter."

The simple statement surprised her and *she* was the one who had said it. Caro looked about the room. Her mother was still in shock. The Count had an expression of dazed puzzlement on his face. The rest of her family and friends looked perplexed. Only Tobias regarded her thoughtfully, so she kept her attention on him.

"Diamonds are supposed to be the hardest natural substance in the world," she continued.

Tobias smiled and she took a step towards him.

"That *wasn't* the real Star of December!"

His smile turned into a grin and she took another step forward, adding a slightly accusing note to her voice.

"*That* was the decoy."

Behind her the Count gasped. She felt rather than saw everyone's eyes on her and Tobias.

He straightened himself and shook out his arms. With his right hand, he tugged at his left sleeve.

"There's nothing up here..."

Then he tugged his right cuff with his left hand.

"...and nothing up here, so..."

He touched her ear with his right hand.

"...you must have it."

He drew back his hand and there in his palm was the Star of December diamond in all its blue, shimmering, *genuine* glory.

"*Mon Dieu!* How...?" asked the Count who was now straightening himself on the chair. Caro observed the colour beginning to return to his visage.

"I palmed the real gem and slipped the fake into the top of the box as you were returning it to the safe after the performance. I knew that would be the only time the diamond would be unattended. It made sense that Pavel and Nemec would try to grab it then."

Walter slapped Tobias on the back. "That was an excellent plan, son, but I wish you'd let me on it. I nearly had a heart attack when that stone shattered!"

"I was just wondering..." interjected Margaret. "Who's staying in this room?"

"I think Pavel and Nemec were," replied Walter. "Why?"

"I was wondering if perhaps the Longmuir Hotel has been the gang's headquarters all along."

"If so," Gwen added with growing excitement. "Does that mean everything stolen by The Phantom is in this room? And if so, where is Van Dyke?"

CHAPTER SIXTEEN

"It was most unfair that your uncle wouldn't let us stay for the search at the hotel," said Margaret as she reached for another strip of coloured paper in yellow. Caro picked up a strip of paper in pink, threaded it through a circlet and glued down the ends to create a new link in the paper chain.

Beside her, Gwen had just finished wrapping gifts, finishing each one with a pretty red and gold ribbon. She reached for a handful of bright red glass berries and soft white satin berries attached to copper wire to work on making extra centrepieces for the table.

Caro had been told this morning there would be extras for dinner, so a fourth leaf would have to be dropped into the dining table to accommodate them all.

"Well, Uncle Walter said it was so as not to taint the evidence," she said. "I really think he wanted to be sure we didn't slip away with any souvenirs from our adventure."

The door to the drawing room opened, bringing with it the scent of pine as Edward, Bertie and the footman wrestled the Christmas tree through the doorway. Edward kicked a box sitting on the floor. Glass ornaments rattled ominously.

"Careful there, sir!" said the footman.

Caro watched them manoeuvre the tree into its cast iron stand. Edward bent down to tighten the clamps to hold the trunk in place. Then the three left with as much noise as they had entered.

"Caro?"

She started at the sound of her name.

Gwen shook her head and smiled at Margaret.

"Caro's been wool gathering all day," she said with an affectionate tease in her voice. "After so much adventure, she must be finding the prospect of an ordinary Christmas rather dull."

"Ah," added Margaret. "That must be it, because I've never ever seen you glum around the holidays, Caro dear."

She glanced up at them but didn't say anything. She continued making her paper chain. It wasn't going to be an ordinary Christmas, was it? At any time between now and the arrival of their other guests, she and Bertie would sit down and have a serious conversation about their future.

He would pull out the ring – most likely the sapphire one – go down on bended knee and ask if she would do him the honour of 'making him the happiest man in England'.

What should she do?

The husband she wanted would be clever, intrepid, fun and resourceful. She supposed Bertie *could* be those things, or some of them perhaps, but in her heart, she knew he was not really. He was kind and faithful and would love her, and she could learn to love him, she supposed, but not in the way she yearned to because he was, well... *Bertie.*

And unfortunately, over the past two weeks, every time she thought of the type of man she wanted to marry, he looked suspiciously like Mr Tobias Black – who was, by now, half way at least to Lancashire by train to spend Christmas with his family. And who knew? Perhaps there was a sweetheart waiting for him there.

The more she thought about it, the more depressed she became. Even the thought of their annual Christmas Eve dinner party wasn't enough to buoy her mood.

Every year a group of the Addison's closest friends gathered at their home for a dinner party. It had become quite the tradition. Everyone would exchange light-hearted gifts and break open the Christmas crackers before heading off to church for midnight Mass. The family would then spend Christmas Day at home where more personal gifts would be exchanged.

Of all the presents she could give to her mother, the acceptance of a marriage proposal would be the greatest. *Oh, Bertie.*

Oh, Tobias...

The three of them had fallen into silence and Caro felt guilty at being the cause of it. She determined to pull herself out of her funk and restore their Christmas cheer. She drew in a deep breath.

"Well, I can tell you one thing," she said. "Mr Hargreaves, the jeweller, had the diamond butterfly brooch back on display today."

"They found it!" Gwen exclaimed and gave a little clap.

"Did they find everything?" asked Margaret.

"I'm not sure," Caro answered. "Uncle Walter is sending his men to every jewellery fence in the city."

"Fence?" Margaret laughed. "I swear Caro, you ought to write some of these things down. You might not be able to practice law when you graduate, but you could tell a jolly good detective story."

"I agree," Gwen piped up. "You'd be awfully good at it."

"Really?" Caro asked, intrigued. "I'd never given it a thought."

"'The young woman who helped Scotland Yard capture The Phantom brings her true life adventures to print'," Gwen said stretching out her arms like an impresario. "No publisher could resist the story of a brave *female* detective. It's never been done before and it's about time it *was*."

This time Caro's grin wasn't forced. "I think you're right. I should!"

The more she thought about it, the possibilities danced in her head more enticingly than sugar plum fairies.

"I think I shall call the first one *The Magician's Secret* and start on it immediately in the New Year."

The rest of the afternoon passed quickly with Margaret and Gwen adding suggestions to her first detective story while they worked on decorating the tree. By the time the large gold star had been placed at the top, Caro's mind was filled with settings, characters and an absolute corker of a plot.

* * *

"Caro?"

She turned at the sound of her name.

"Are you alone?"

There was a *look* in Bertie's puppy dog eyes, an earnestness, an excitement she had never before seen in her dear friend.

"Yes. Gwen and Margaret have gone upstairs to dress for dinner."

She swallowed the lump in her throat as he took her hands and led her to the fireplace. He paused as though searching for the right words to say.

"We've known each other for years, haven't we?"

"At least twenty," she agreed.

"And you know I hold you in the deepest regard. You're as much a part of *my* family as I am!"

Caro couldn't help the heat running up her cheeks.

"Well, I'm about to ask the most important question a man can ever ask, and I need your honest answer."

The lump in her throat descended to her ribs, making it impossible to take in a full lungful of air. He released her hands. She watched, as though in a dream, while he pulled out of his jacket pocket a small velvet covered ring box.

"I took your advice back in the jewellery store and picked the ring that most reminded me of the woman I want to give it to."

He opened the hinged lid and inside was the beautiful Alexandrite and seed pearl ring, the blues and greens shimmering in the prism of pink stone.

"Do you think Margaret will like it?"

What little air remained in Caro's lungs came out with a *whoosh*.

"You're going to ask *Margaret* to marry you?" Her question was little more than a whisper.

"Yes!" And this time it was Bertie's turn to blush. "On New Year's Eve."

"Oh, *Bertie!*"

"I spoke to her father last week. He told me my affection for Margaret was not unrequited. But I know how close you two are and I wanted you to know and give you my solemn vow that I will make her happy, always."

Tears danced at the edge of her lashes and she reached out to take his hands in hers.

"*Dear* Bertie, I was so blind not to see the affection you and Margaret have always had for one another. You will make each other very happy. I know it."

Caro blinked away the tears of joy before kissing him on the cheek.

"First Edward and Gwen, and now my two best friends in all the world are getting married. This is the most wonderful Christmas ever!"

CHAPTER SEVENTEEN

Caro circled the dining table, adding place cards as her mother directed. She mentally tallied up the number of guests invited to dinner.

"Do we know who the extra place is for?" she asked.

"Hmmm?" Her mother looked up over the list. "It's someone Walter asked to invite. I'm not entirely sure who it is but I have my suspicions."

Hearing the conspiratorial tone in her mother's voice, Caro matched it. "*Mother*... you can't keep me in suspense."

Her mother smiled and lowered her voice. "A little while ago, Walter happened to mention a widow he admired."

"You think he's considering marrying again?"

"I don't know and he didn't say, but he asked to bring a guest and I agreed. It also makes us fourteen – and you know how I dislike thirteen at the table. It's *so* unlucky."

"So where shall we seat this mysterious friend of Uncle Walter's?"

Estelle Addison cast her eye across the table.

"Seat her... across from you, next to Sir Hubert," she said.

Caro duly placed the card marked 'Guest' into the ornate silver placeholder shaped like a Christmas tree.

After Bertie's news, Caro had determined the party was going to be especially festive, and even more so now particularly if Uncle Walter was going to introduce his lady friend to the family.

She stood back and looked at the setting. She loved their Christmas table. On the crisp white table cloth stood tall candelabras. The table salts were whimsical silver sleighs pulled by reindeer. The dinner plates were edged in gold and decorated with bright green holly leaves and scarlet red berries around the rim. The matching dinner service had been in the family for years and was only brought out for the festive season.

Beside each place with its silver tree placeholder was one of Tom Smith's Finest Christmas Crackers, each a different colour and filled with a little silver trinket, an amusing joke and a silly hat. They had become somewhat of a tradition at Christmas Eve dinner.

* * *

The Gilfroys were the first to arrive. Sir Hubert was as exuberant as ever, his wife less so which Sir Hubert explained was a result of a slight headache. The young woman sat in a darkened corner away from the polyphon which Edward had wound up to play one of the new discs just arrived from Germany, Stille Nacht, Heilige Nacht – *Silent Night, Holy Night* – very appropriate for Christmas.

Caro spoke to all the guests in turn – sharing a joke with Bertie's father, a little bit of society gossip with Gwen's mother and Margaret's mother – all the while watching Margaret and Bertie trying not to make their interest in each other too plain.

Now they were waiting for was Uncle Walter and his guest.

"Do you think Margaret is the only one not to know?" asked Caro softly as she handed Gwen a glass of sherry.

"Oh, I think she knows, or is hopeful at least, but she'd never say anything, certainly not to Bertie and never to us."

"He showed me the ring," said Caro and she couldn't help let a little pride enter her voice. "In fact, I helped him pick it out."

"You didn't!" said Gwen. She lowered her voice and might have said more if not for the announcement of another guest.

Caro turned, expecting to greet Uncle Walter and his lady friend but instead came face-to-face with Tobias Black.

Their eyes met and held for a moment before he turned away to accept her father's hearty hand shake.

"Mr Black, what an unexpected surprise!" said Mr Addison. "I take it you're our fourteenth. Walter's running late and he didn't leave many details, it was very last minute..."

"Do please call me Tobias," he laughed, "and indeed sir, I suspected that to be the case. It was a last minute invitation to me too. I had planned to leave for Lancashire this afternoon, but Inspector Addison asked me specifically to come, so thank you for making me feel welcome."

"Not at all, not at all. Caro, will you arrange a drink while I introduce Tobias to the rest of our party?"

From the drinks table, Caro watched Tobias join in the conversation as though he had been lifelong friends with everyone in the room, though she noticed he glanced her way as he said hello again to Edward and Bertie.

She went over and handed him his drink – and the smile he gave her as she did so made her feel weak at the knees.

At long last, after answering everyone's questions about his future plans, the magic show, and being asked to recount once again his brave dash along the ledge of the Longmuir Hotel, he approached her.

"It's great to see you again, Caro."

She swore she didn't mistake the warmth in his voice – or the heat of her own cheeks.

"And you too," she answered before dropping her voice. "Do you really have no idea why Uncle Walter invited you tonight?"

"I wish I did. I'd like to think it's my charm and wit, but it's more likely to be unfinished business."

"About The Phantom case?"

"Uh-huh. And something about it has been bothering me too."

"Like what?"

Caro became aware of someone else entering the room.

"Sorry I'm late everyone, official police business," said Walter, shrugging his shoulders, his apology being explanation enough.

There seemed to be a watchful edge to her uncle tonight as though he were on duty. When she glanced up at Tobias, she saw he wore a slight frown.

"What's he up to?" he muttered softly, almost to himself it seemed.

The dinner gong sounded.

"Well, whatever it is will have to wait until after dinner," she said, accepting his arm.

* * *

When they had finished at table, Caro excused herself and rushed up to her room. They would soon be opening their gifts, mere trifles really – a handkerchief, a box of chocolates, a note book – just a token, but it only seemed right that Tobias receive a gift too.

She pulled out the chartreuse scarf – the one he had discarded all those weeks ago in the pursuit to the station and she had yet to return it to him. She smiled as she wrapped it in a piece of plain brown paper, secured with one of her green hair ribbons. It seemed fitting to return it to him this way – a little misdirection of her own.

By the time she returned down stairs, her father had started distributing gifts. She'd missed the start but saw Uncle Walter with a new tobacco pouch, there was a note book each for herself and Margaret, a stationery set for Gwen.

Caro found Tobias standing by the fire, slightly apart from the group.

"You don't miss out," she said, offering the beribboned package. He looked surprised.

"You have to open it now, Black. It's the family tradition," Edward called.

Tobias inclined his head and slipped the ribbon off the paper. The look of delight as he recognised his own scarf endeared him to Caro even more.

"What a ghastly colour," Bertie exclaimed. "Caro, where on earth did you get such a monstrosity?"

The look Tobias shared with her made plain it was *her* choice to keep its origin a secret or not.

Aware now all eyes were on her, she simply offered an enigmatic smile.

"*That* is a long story, which will have to wait for another time."

The clock struck ten, the full sounding gong resonating throughout the house.

Walter cleared his throat to draw everyone's attention.

"Before we all go on to church tonight, I just wanted to say a few words. I invited Tobias here tonight, first of all to offer the thanks of the Metropolitan Police for his assistance at not inconsiderable risk to himself," said Uncle Walter.

Tobias gave a theatrical bow in response to the compliment and the subsequent applause.

"I know," continued Walter, "you're all very interested in knowing the upshot of our investigation and, because you have also been involved with the case, I'm going to give you an off the record briefing... There are no reporters here, are there?"

Everyone laughed at Walter's joke.

"We have Caro's fine work in deducing how our thieves entered the jewellery store in the Barrington Arcade. Her observation – and, dare I say it, perseverance – led to our first solid piece of evidence in tying our two acrobats to the crime – the cigar band carelessly discarded in the floor space between the solicitor's office and the jewellery store.

"We traced the cigars back to Lord Howarth who reported them stolen a few weeks earlier, along with the Howarth family diamonds. These facts led us to our elaborate stakeout, the successful protection of the Star of December diamond, and the capture of Pavel and Nemec. From being pilloried in the press, Scotland Yard now gets praise and a special commendation from the Chief Commissioner which is Christmas gift enough for me.

"I'm also delighted to satisfy curiosity on a subject I know the young ladies of my acquaintance are particularly interested in…"

Caro, Gwen and Margaret looked at one another and grinned.

"And that is whether the stolen diamonds have been recovered. Apparently, the plan was for Van Dyke to meet our two thieves on the Isle of Jersey for the final payment and hand over of the gems.

"I can tell you that all the diamonds have been recovered–"

Everyone gasped and burst into spontaneous applause, yet Caro noticed Sir Hubert, usually so ebullient, was pale and appeared to be holding his breath.

Uncle Walter pulled out his pipe and touched a taper on the fire to light it. Blue smoke rose upward on each puff as he waited until the room had quietened.

"–except for one suite."

Caro saw how Sir Hubert was suddenly the focus of her uncle's attention. She watched the peer release a long slow breath, his pale face beginning to recover some of its colour.

Lady Constance, who had said little all evening, dabbed a handkerchief to her eyes.

"In fact," said Walter, "our pair of villains deny emphatically they took that particular set of jewels."

"Well they would, wouldn't they?" Sir Hubert replied crisply. "Why would you believe them?"

"I'm inclined to believe them because of something Tobias said."

Caro sensed Tobias come to attention beside her.

"Sir Hubert," said Walter, "were any cigars stolen from your home?"

"No. Only the jewels."

"Just as I thought. There was one fact omitted from the papers and that was at least a handful of cigars – in some cases a whole box – were stolen from each of the targeted households as well as the jewels.

"I'm not sure I follow, Inspector," said Tobias.

Walter took a puff from his pipe, then pointed the stem in Tobias's direction. "You mentioned the criminals seemed to be stealing to order. Indeed, in each case, The Phantom – or should I say Phantoms? – were following a list given them by Van Dyke.

"Everything we recovered was on that list. Everything but the Catherine the Great jewels – which were *not* on the list. And another thing that bothered me – and

Caro saw it too – was the thieves made such a mess in Sir Hubert's bedroom, what with the open safe door, jewellery trays and papers strewn everywhere, the broken glass in the garden bed below...

"Pavel and Nemec were quite insulted – they said they're professionals who pride themselves in leaving no trace."

"Well, if it wasn't the Phantom, then some other thief must have stolen them," protested Sir Hubert, a defensive note now entering his voice. "It happened the night of the ball. Hundreds of people were in the house."

"We spoke to your butler. He said you told him to make sure the staff was extra vigilant that no guests accessed the family quarters."

Sir Hubert's previously pale face was now beet red. "What are you insinuating, Walter?"

The Inspector took a puff of his pipe once again before answering.

"I think you know," he said, his voice revealing the gravity of the allegation as yet unspoken. "The theft of your gems has all the hallmarks of an inside job. We've done some investigating. The insurance payout would help cover some of the losses in your business, wouldn't it?"

Caro's mother gasped softly and looked at her husband. James took her hand and patted it, shaking his head sadly. The young people, however, were openly agog.

"You know how to kick a man when he's low," answered Sir Hubert, his voice now a snarl. "Yes! My business is struggling, and now you accuse me of *this!*"

Walter kept his tone soft and even. "We've taken a look at the books and we're looking to trace a series of regular payments to a company in Austria going back more than twelve months. And you recently booked an open ended trip to the continent leaving on New Year's Eve, didn't you?"

"This is outrageous!"

There was silence in the drawing room. No one dared speak.

"Hubert," said Lady Constance at last, her kerchief nothing but a screwed up ribbon. "I told you this wouldn't work."

"Shut up, shut up!"

"You!" Sir Hubert pointed a finger at Walter. His hand shook, knuckles white. "You have no proof."

"I hold enough suspicion to have the Home Office cancel your passport and that of your wife."

"Without the diamonds, you have nothing!"

Tobias cleared his throat and stepped forward.

"Countess, I see you've not opened your gift," he said.

"I... I want to save it for Christmas Day," she said, holding the small package closer.

"I wrapped that gift, Mr Black," said Gwen. Edward took her hand and looked at his uncle, questioningly.

Walter nodded to acknowledge the young woman, but he turned his attention back to Tobias. "What are you thinking?"

"I'm thinking if we unwrap it, we'll see something interesting," Tobias replied.

Walter turned to Lady Constance. "Madam?"

With a venomous glance at her husband, the beautiful young woman untied the ribbon carefully, unfolding the crisp red, green and gold Christmas paper with great deliberation. Then she slowly lifted the lid on the box.

Sitting amongst the wrapped chocolates were diamonds, round, pear shaped and emerald cut, some of them still connected to the platinum wires that had once made them Catherine the Great's necklace.

EPILOGUE

T he clock in the hall striking half-past eleven seemed much louder tonight, perhaps because the silence had become so deafening in the drawing room after Walter's revelation. He had left quietly with Sir Hubert and Lady Constance.

Now the others, more or less equally subdued, were in the hallway getting ready for midnight Mass. Only Caro and Tobias remained in the drawing room.

Tobias looked at the closed door, seeming torn over what to do next.

"Perhaps I should catch up with Inspector Addison," he said.

Caro touched his sleeve.

"My uncle has everything well in hand, I'm sure," she said.

"I feel I'm responsible for ruining your family's Christmas."

"You have done no such thing," Caro reassured him. "I think we're all in a bit of shock. We've known the Gilfroys for years."

She let out a sigh full of regret and tugged the bell pull. "If only Sir Hubert had come to anyone of our families when he was in difficulties... but justice must be done and it should always be no respecter of persons."

The butler arrived to her summons and left again on Caro's instruction to have a footman prepare the gig to take Tobias to Victoria Station. There he would catch the midnight mail train to Lancashire.

"You didn't tell me much about your family," she said.

"I told my mother I would be home on Christmas Day this year, and I can just manage to make good on my promise. I'll arrive home just before everyone sits down for breakfast – my mother, father and elder brother and his wife, and their three boys. Little terrors." He smiled. "No, actually they're great boys. I enjoy being their uncle."

"They sound wonderful," she said and couldn't help feel the hollowness in her chest as she prepared herself to say good bye.

This time for good.

For the sake of her peace of mind she had to change the subject. "How did you know the diamonds were in the box of chocolates?"

"The bows on the gifts were all tied a particular way which told me it was the work of one person. The one for Lady Constance was the first on the console table which was how I noticed it particularly. I happened to look again after dinner and noticed the bow was different, as if it had been rewrapped, and it was the only one that looked different. So when she hadn't opened it as everyone else had done with their gifts, I made an educated guess."

Caro shook her head in awe.

"I'm going to miss you, Tobias Black. You never cease to amaze me."

There was something in his eyes, a spark of something Caro couldn't dare to imagine.

"I think that's a better gift than the return of my scarf because I was hoping... I'll be back in London a few days after New Year's Day, may I call on you?"

"Yes. Oh, most definitely yes!"

The full smile on Tobias's face she knew was the twin to the expression on her own.

He took her hands and brought them to his lips.

Caro held her breath. Memories of Christmas one year ago with Bertie's disappointing kiss under the mistletoe came back in a rush. But this was different, her entire body seemed electrified. Even her lips tingled.

Tobias leaned closer and Caro's eyes closed before his lips touched hers – and when they did it was soft, warm and full of promise.

It was everything she imagined a true love's kiss to be.

In fact, it was magic.

THE END

Three Ships

A Note From The Author

Three *Ships* was written for the free eBook anthology *A Season To Remember: Four Short Stories For Christmas* and first published in 2014. It is a light hearted romantic adventure.

The anthology contains three other titles from fellow authors Susanne Bellamy, Noelle Clark and Eva Scott. It is available from Smashwords.com

Chapter One

I saw three ships come sailing in
On Christmas Day, on Christmas Day;
I saw three ships come sailing in
On Christmas Day in the morning.

"Goin' to be a bad storm, Miss Laura. I can feel it in me bones, I can." Mr Fletcher pointed a thumb at the barometer hung on his wall. Even without reference to the brass and rosewood instrument that was the man's pride and joy, Laura knew him to be correct.

There were other signs — the shift in the on-shore breeze and the way the clouds banked on the horizon.

"Indeed it will be," she agreed, handing over a list. "Which is why I want to get more provisions, in case we're cut off from the mainland for more than a day or two."

"Not good just afore Christmas," the grocer observed, taking her list.

The middle-aged shop keeper, his starched white apron stretched over an expansive belly, scanned the piece of paper.

"Dickie!" he called in a booming voice, "Come out here and fetch these items for Miss Laura."

Richard Wells poked his head out from the back store room. Dickie to everyone at Ashton-On-Sea, and rarely seen dressed in other than his customary faded overalls, smiled at Laura and took the list from his boss.

"Be sure to pack it up nice and good, mind," Mr Fletcher admonished before turning back to his customer. "You'll be wanting Mrs Parker's home-made apricot preserves as well, I dare say?"

"Yes, please."

"Three?" the grocer asked hopefully.

Sly old fox! Laura smiled to herself.

She shook her head.

"Just one will be fine, Dickie."

From behind Mr Fletcher, Dickie offered an approving grin.

"Be ready for you in an hour Miss Laura," he answered before setting to work to fill her order.

Laura thanked the men and left the shop, the little brass bell on the door tinkling as it closed.

Laura Winter paused to look out towards her home.

The view half a mile out to St Joseph's Rock was one she never tired of — the pile of sea darkened rocks at its base, the solid mound of rock topped with grass from which the lighthouse rose, gleaming white, its mullion windows sparkling in the mid-morning sunlight. It was home and she considered it with not a little pride.

According to local legend, St Joseph's Rock was the place where Joseph of Arimathea landed in England, accompanied by Jesus as a young man.

Laura doubted the story herself, but ever since the verse by that poet William Blake was published a few years ago, visitors aplenty had come to their corner of the Devon coast during each Summer season.

Thus the legend grew and was embellished by the entrepreneurial townsfolk who supplemented their fishing income by making souvenirs.

Though bright, the late November day carried a chill and Laura turned her face up to the sun to feel its warmth on her cheeks. She balanced the wicker basket on her arm and brushed a strand of red-gold hair from her face.

The clock on the nearby church tower chimed the tenth hour but her musings were interrupted by Reverend Harman. He had been a boxer before taking holy orders and, although older now and a little softer around the middle, he still carried a fighter's physique.

The cleric fell in step with her as she walked down the main street of Ashton-On-Sea, its rows of Tudor-era buildings huddled together as if against the sometimes harsh weather, just as they had done for three hundred years.

"How's your father, Miss Laura?" he enquired. "I paid a visit with him earlier this week and he assured me his foot was well on the mend. Choir practice hasn't been the same without him."

"Stubborn as always!" she exclaimed with equal measures of affection and exasperation. "I finally managed to persuade him to let me check the light twice a day, but he still insists on climbing those stairs to wind the clockwork. Only Mother could persuade him to take care of himself."

Reverend Harman offered a sympathetic smile in memory of Laura's mother who died five years ago, when she was only fifteen.

"Well you only just have to ask if there is anything you need," he reminded her. "So don't be stubborn like your father if you want help."

The mild admonishment of his words was softened with a smile.

"Yoohoo, Reverend!"

They turned at the call.

Across the street Mrs Merriwether waved. She was a large woman with an equally substantial bosom and reminded Laura of a beautifully beribboned figure eight.

Next to her, Miss Jones, the school mistress, thin and reed-like, remained at her shoulder. Her no-nonsense expression quailed many a schoolboy into obedience yet beneath that hawk-like expression lay a character with an equally sharp sense of humour.

"Oh Reverend," called Mrs Merriwether, "we need to talk to you about some last minute preparations for the Christmas fete."

"Hello Laura!" she continued. "Thank you for the beautiful quilts, I'm sure they'll fetch a great price for this year's charity."

Laura accepted the thanks and excused herself. Living on a tidal island had its advantages and one of them was the ability to graciously take leave from drawn-out conversations by pointing to the change of tide.

Indeed, St Joseph's Rock was quite accessible via the causeway at low tide but completely cut-off during high tide and the storm surges that regularly battered the exposed coast.

And in truth out to sea, clouds as dark as bruises were gathering, edging the horizon as a sharp gust of breeze cut up the promontory. Even at this distance, Laura could see the flag by the lighthouse snap to attention.

By the time the church bells chimed one o'clock, she had returned to Fletcher's Fine Emporium to find Dickie loading the last of her order onto the small horse-drawn cart.

"Mr Fletcher asked, what with your dad laid up with a bung foot and you there on St Joseph's on your own like...well, if you need a man about, he said I should go with you."

Try as he might, Dickie could not hide the hint of a frown on his brow and Laura recognised its cause immediately.

"That's very sweet of you," she said, causing Dickie to blush, "but I know Kitty has been waiting for you to take her to the dance this Friday and she would be most disappointed if you didn't go."

The young man's face lit up.

"You're a real friend, Miss Laura. Anything you need, don't be afraid to ask now. It would be my pleasure."

It was not until she was crossing the causeway in the cart that she allowed herself a gentle laugh at Dickie's delight in not being prised away from his sweetheart. The thought caused her to reflect.

It was only in the past year she'd pondered the notion of having a beau of her own and her mind idly considered those eligible as she negotiated the path home.

Not that there were many eligible. The fight against Napoleon's armies had occupied and taken many a young man. Those who remained were more like brothers to her. Laura couldn't see herself accepting a proposal from any one of them, even if they should offer.

The muted clip-clop on the cobble-paved causeway cut through her thoughts. The tide was rising faster than it usually did and the horse sloshed hoof deep along the path said to have been laid by the last of the Saxon rulers.

No, she decided, the man for her must be dashing, but kind; intelligent, but with a sense of humour; brave and handsome.

Where on earth would she meet such a paragon in a small seaside town? One would simply have to fall into her lap.

Chapter Two

By the time the horse and cart had negotiated the tight, steep turns up the path to the top of St Joseph's Rock, small waves were breaking over the causeway. Laura looked at the sky ahead, a crisp formation of arcus cloud approached like the advancing tide, heading for the coast.

"Papa, I'm home," she called, her arms filled with the first of two small crates. There was no answer, but that didn't alarm her. His badly-sprained foot wouldn't stop him hauling himself up the one hundred and eight steps to the top of the tower to use his telescope and check his barometer, to take notes on the storm to come.

Laura set the load on the kitchen table of their cottage and called from the bottom of the stairwell that led up to the light.

"Papa?"

"You're back, dear girl!" a voice echoed down the void. "Just one more measurement and I'll be right down to give you a hand."

Laura grinned and shook her head.

By the time he had managed to get downstairs, she would have brought in all of their provisions and unharnessed Acorn. Not that she minded. Laura took an interest in her father's weather recordings — those measures of the scale and scope of the weather influenced the livelihood of everyone in the district.

And indeed she was correct. By the time her father joined her, Laura had begun the heavy weather routine her father had taught her as a child — persuade Milly the goat into her pen, chase the chickens back into their coop inside the stone-walled courtyard, then take a walk around the perimeter of the lighthouse and its cottage to close the storm shutters.

The sound of a timber door slamming against the stone wall alerted her to her father's arrival downstairs.

She hurried around the lee of the building to find him outside and struggling to manage his crutches and the heavy cloak laid across his left arm.

Peter Winter, despite ruddy and weathered features that were testament to a life dedicated to the sea, was a still handsome man in his early fifties. He shared his daughter's bright green eyes and ready smile.

"I don't know who is supposed be looking after who here," he said, offering her the garment.

Laura accepted it and was grateful for its warmth.

Walking side-by-side, they abandoned the protection of the lighthouse walls to venture closer to the southern end of St Joseph's Rock. Spray reached them even at that height as waves whipped up by the coming storm crashed and broke apart on the massive black boulders below.

Laura was about to make comment when she found her father staring straight out to sea. She folded her arm into her father's and looked out to sea also. The storm clouds edged closer and heavy rain fell like a black curtain across the grey sea about a mile away from the shore.

"There's a boat out there," she said.

"Aye," he muttered more to himself than her, "but there was two a couple of hours ago."

"Together?" she asked, but her voice was carried away unheard in the rising wind.

Laura's father turned and hobbled back towards the lighthouse, moving swiftly on his crutches. Laura glanced back at the sea. Silhouetted by a flash of lightning, a ketch battled the increased swell.

She followed swiftly towards the lighthouse, noticing the sharp splinters of afternoon sunlight still falling inland, a reminder of the changeable weather on the Devon coast.

No sooner had the door slammed behind her than her father called.

"You'll have to give me a hand, love," he called down from towards the top of the stairs which he had ascended backwards on hand and seat with his bandaged foot straight out in front.

His crutches were propped at the bottom of the stairs and the edge to his voice spurred her on. Her father rarely asked for help.

The clatter of her footsteps on the iron treads competed with a roll of thunder. Laura reached the light tower just a few steps behind her father and helped him to stand so he could half-hop, half-limp about the room.

As she lit the wicks for the lamp, she could hear the clank-clank sound of the clockwork mechanism being wound. She closed the lens and, with a clunk as her father engaged the mechanism, the large lantern started to rotate, sending shards of light through the panes of glass that could be seen miles out to sea.

"Do you think it was one of our boats?" she asked, breathless from the burst of activity.

The fishing fleet at Ashton-On-Sea was one of the main livelihoods in the town but she knew a vessel lost on the rocks of St Joseph's would mean more than economic loss.

"I don't know," her father admitted. "I thought I counted all the fleet in about an hour ago. I hope whoever it is so foolhardy to have been caught up in the storm makes it to port before the worst hits."

As the lantern lens swept around again, she could see the firm set of his jaw and tight, worried lines around his eyes.

"This is going to be a big one," he said. "I can't ever recall the barometer dropping so quickly."

The wind died down as though the storm was holding its breath for a moment. It was an eerie sort of calm. Lightning heralded what was to come.

One-one thousand, two-one thousand, three-one thousand, four...

Crack!

The thunder snapped and popped, the sound echoing noisily in the centre of the lighthouse tower.

Then the rains came, hard driving torrential rain that beat against the shutters, demanding entrance.

The returned wind howled and rose.

"You go below, love," said her father, "I'll be right behind you."

Downstairs, Laura lit a lamp and set it on the kitchen table before tending to the fire in the hearth in preparation for making dinner.

Thunder rumbled overhead once more, and Admiral and Whisky the cats, one black and the other brown, scampered in to sit by the warmth of the fire and to eye any tidbits that might drop to the floor at mealtime.

The frequent Atlantic storms had ceased to frighten Laura many years ago. The stone walls and storm shutters protected them from the elements, though tonight the shutters rattled on their hinges by wind looking for ingress.

Nonetheless, Laura had a little ritual that gave her confidence in the face of the most ferocious tempests. It was silly really, but she felt better for doing it. As she began to chop the vegetables for the evening meal, she looked around the kitchen.

On one of the two blue-painted Welsh dressers were bottles of neatly labelled antiseptics, and crisp new bandages wound and stacked in tidy rows along with other medical miscellany. They stood like little soldiers at attention, waiting to be called to duty.

She surveyed them at a glance then looked over to the rear door. By it, a key hung on a brass loop. It opened the storage shed at the far end of the courtyard, where ropes, pulleys and nets were kept in good order to help rescue the crew of foundering vessels. Stores of powder were held there too — blue light for flares, black powder for the signal cannon — and all were assiduously checked every month.

Laura heard the clatter of her father taking up his crutches in the stairwell at last just as lightning once more flashed overhead. The accompanying crack of thunder was near deafening.

Despite his name, Admiral wasn't very brave; neither was his sister. Both cats beat a hasty retreat under one of the dressers.

Laura and her father were as prepared as they possibly could be. Hopefully it would be enough should the boat they had seen be driven on the rocks.

Sometime in the early hours of the morning, the storm abated.

Despite being hampered by his injury, Laura's father was already up and outside in the still gusting winds, opening the storm shutters. Little by little, a pale rosy light filled the parlour and the kitchen.

Red sky in the morning, sailor's warning.

He had hung the kettle over the kitchen fire too and it was beginning to boil when Laura entered the room. She quickly prepared a steaming hot mug of tea and took it out her father. He exchanged one of his crutches for it and gamely held the mug in one hand as he limped over to check the storage shed.

Laura released the chickens which spilled pell-mell from their coop to peck at the wind-whipped grass, little bothered by the two cats that playfully stalked them, and went to milk Milly. Afterwards, the goat gambolled out on to the grass, bleating her appreciation.

Laura took the milk inside and emerged again with a small telescope.

"I'm going to check the cliff edges," she called to her father, waving the spyglass. He was now at the stable door and raised a hand in acknowledgement.

She started with her favourite view, one which looked back to Ashton-On-Sea, but this morning the view was not good.

Several vessels had broken their moorings and were bobbing unmanned in the roiling sea inside Ashton Quay. Some dinghies were now little more than matchwood, first washed ashore then pushed further onto The Strand by waves that breached the sea wall by several feet even as she watched.

Not surprisingly, the causeway was completely submerged and would likely be so for several days. Spumes of white flecks shot many feet up in the air, filling the atmosphere with salty brine.

St Joseph's Rock was now an isolated island, only a quarter of a mile in area. A small grove of stunted trees, tenaciously gripping the Rock, formed a natural wind break on the western side. Laura edged around them to peer thirty feet down to where, in fine weather, a small sandy beach would be.

Something caught her eye. As a wave receded, the shape resolved itself.

It was not piece of flotsam but the body of a man, face down on a large boulder.

Chapter Three

Laura's father watched her shoulder the long coil of rope. "I'm not happy, dear girl. I should be the one going down there, not you."

She gave a pointed look at his injured foot. The way down to the beach was not sheer but it was no gentle slope either and the footing would be treacherous. "Well, needs must," she replied firmly. "I'll be back quickly."

His response was a grimace. He secured the trailing end of the coiled rope to Acorn's saddle.

"Watch your step, Laura," he admonished.

Trailing the rope out as she went, Laura picked her way down the side of the hill with care where the low-growing grass was slick. She grew up here and knew the cliffs well enough to treat them with respect. The saltiness from exploding waves filled her nostrils. She could even taste it on the back of her throat.

The beach filled and emptied as the waves churned in.

She scrambled over one rock, then around another to reach the man. The hem of her skirt darkened in the splashing water.

Still a few feet away, she called out.

"Sailor! Sailor, ahoy!"

The man remained still.

Laura looked back up the thirty feet to where her father peered back, concerned. He called to her but his words were ripped away by the wind.

Her only choice was to approach the man.

The sailor's shirt was torn and shredded, the sodden fabric dark and clinging to the contours of his back. His black hair whipped in the wind like the damp grass around the chickens.

She touched his cheek. His skin was cold.

It might already be too late!

Laura drew a deep breath and grasped his shoulders.

"Come on sailor, time to wake up," she said hopefully, shaking him.

The man obliged her with a groan; Laura matched it with a sigh of relief.

"Help is here," she said.

The man raised himself to his elbows and looked blearily at her. It was hard to determine his age. He seemed much younger than her father but older than Dickie Wells.

"Where are you hurt? Your back? Your legs?"

The man sat up gingerly, shaking his head at each question.

"We're going to haul you out," she said.

The man looked her up and down and flashed her a quick smile, his pale blue eyes twinkling with sudden merriment.

"My guardian angel..." he rasped, interrupted by a hacking cough. "Where is the rest of your heavenly choir?"

"It's just me and my father," she said, pointing up the cliff.

She shucked off the remaining coils of rope and looped the end under his arms, tying it around his chest to create a harness.

Despite his ordeal, the man seemed well enough, and fit too — his shoulders broad and muscles firm around his arms.

He tried to rise to his feet but stumbled. Laura caught his wrist to support him and he hissed in pain.

She glanced down and saw his wrist had been rubbed red raw. The man shook off her hand, ignoring her scrutiny and whistled sharply towards her father on the cliff.

The mysterious stranger limped across the rocks to a grassy area as Laura's father drove Acorn to take up the slack and then, with a jolt, the rope tautened and he began to climb the steep hill, supported by the rope.

Guardian angel... Laura shook her head. With the speed he was making his way up the cliff, the sailor was the one who seemed to have wings.

However, it also appeared he had sense enough to realise how weakened he was. He had not refused the assistance of the rope — which, Laura reflected, might as easily have being used now to haul his lifeless body up the slope — and he stumbled repeatedly, the rope all that prevented him from tumbling back down.

By the time she regained the top, the sailor was on his haunches, recovering his breath as her father untied the rope around his chest.

The man stood, wincing in pain. He was tall, a good inch taller than Laura's father who remained watchful and wary of the man.

An hour or so later, they had learned his name but not much more.

Michael Renten sat hunched on a chair before the kitchen fire, his hands around a mug of tea. His borrowed clothes did not fit well but at least they were clean and dry.

"I couldn't get down to the base of the rock but from what I saw up top there doesn't seem to be any more survivors," Laura's father said after a long period of silence.

"And you're not likely to either, sir."

"I thought that might be the case, Mr Renten."

Laura's father folded his arms and rested against the frame of the door that led to the lighthouse tower. Even on crutches, he was still an imposing figure.

"So would you mind telling us the full story?"

Laura frowned. "We've rescued people from the rocks before, father, and we've never demanded an explanation from them."

Admiral jumped up on the arm of the chair and nudged Laura's shoulder with his head. She stroked him absently.

Her father nodded at their guest.

"This man's wrists were bound together. He could be an escaped convict."

The young man spat out a bitter laugh, looking at his bandaged wrists.

"An elegant deduction from the evidence but completely the wrong conclusion."

"Then explain yourself."

"I am a lieutenant in His Majesty's Waterguard. I was instructed to work in league with a group of blockade runners from Cornwall to identify their ringleader. They made a rendezvous with another vessel yesterday."

With a sigh, the man put down his cup and rubbed his wrists.

"One of the men from the other boat recognised me; a blackguard with whom I once served in His Majesty's Navy," he continued. "The men might have gutted me through then and there, but their leader decided to bind my hands and toss me overboard just as the storm was bearing down."

Laura looked to her father and said nothing. The story seemed plausible.

Renten sighed. "I don't expect you to believe me, but if you sent someone to contact the Customs House at Plymouth..."

"We're completely cut off until the swell has died down," she said before her father silenced her with a cautioning glance.

The young man turned to Laura as if noticing her for the first time. "Indeed, miss?" he responded.

He was a handsome man to be sure. His hair had dried to a rich dark brown and, not bound with a ribbon, it fell to his shoulder.

He gave her a quick smile before turning back to her father.

"Do you have signal flags?" he asked.

The signal of fourteen flags was too long for the flag pole so Laura's father suspended a line from an upper window in the light house to the pole. It read *Authenticate Agent MR.*

As Lieutenant Renten caught up on sleep in a store room hastily turned into quarters, Laura set an extra place at the table for their guest.

"Do you believe his story?" she asked her father. He took his time in answering. "I suppose we'll find out in a few days," he answered in a noncommittal tone.

"I wonder what happened to the other ship."

"Probably long gone, miss. If they were wise, they would have headed out to sea."

Laura jumped at the unexpected voice.

Rested, washed and shaved, the lieutenant looked more handsome than ever. She couldn't help but picture him in his dress uniform, sharply pressed navy blue jacket with white collars and cuffs and bright brass buttons...

Stop it! She rebuked herself and quickly looked away, pretending to find the corned beef cooking in the pot to be particularly fascinating — yet not before she caught a glimpse of amusement in his expression.

The fine late autumn day was drawing to a close and Laura's father hoisted himself up on to his crutches ready to wind the clockwork.

"Can I assist you with the light, sir?" asked Renten.

The lighthouse keeper hesitated.

"A small service to help repay your hospitality," the lieutenant pressed.

The older man accepted and the two ascended the stairs to the light.

The mantle clock in the parlour chimed seven and there was no sign of her father or the lieutenant.

"Where could they have gone?" she asked the cats. Whisky merely blinked at her but Admiral looked sharply toward the door and made an odd little growl.

"Stop it," she said, reprovingly, but she too wondered whether she had heard anything amiss. Admiral gave her a disinterested glance back.

A stiff evening breeze picked up. That would explain it. Admiral stared intently at the door.

"No, you are not going outside."

Laura cast her eye about and saw the scrag ends of the meat that she had set aside.

"Here." She held a piece up for him to see and it met with his approval.

Now that the cats are fed, what about the men?

Laura opened the connecting door to the tower and laughter met her ears as the two men descended.

"I thought I was going to have to send a search party for you two!" she said as they entered the kitchen, but her exasperation was quelled by the pleasure her father was clearly having in the lieutenant's company.

"My fault entirely, dear lady."

Renten bowed formally so she curtsied in response.

"Well, my dear lieutenant, you can make amends by helping me bring the plates to the table."

As they sat down to eat at the kitchen table, Laura heard Milly bleat once outside then stop.

No, it was nothing, she thought. Just the wind.

Chapter four

The evening went splendidly. The lieutenant was convivial company and demonstrated through his actions as well as his words that his claim of rank was not unfounded.

Indeed, he had impressed Laura's father to the extent that he brought out a bottle of port after dinner. The two men stood by the fire with a glass each and Laura sat opposite with some needlework — anything to stop her restless fidgeting.

She watched Lieutenant Renten beneath her lashes.

It would have been lovely to have met him under other circumstances, Laura thought. A tea dance perhaps, where he would be in his dress uniform and she would be in a pink — no, a green, sprigged dress.

He would approach her, bow and say—

"Are you feeling all right, love?"

Laura started.

"I'm sorry, father. I was wool-gathering."

A blush crept up her cheeks and she pointedly kept her face away from their visitor. There was a silence which threatened to be awkward before Renten spoke.

"May I ask what happened to your foot, Mr Winter?"

"Too much Whisky."

"Oh..." said the lieutenant, unsure how otherwise to respond.

Laura held a smile in check at his expression.

Then, as if on cue, a furry, orange-brown streak sped across the room, narrowly missing the man.

"Meet Whisky," said Laura. "Around her, no one is steady on their feet."

And they all joined in the laughter.

As the evening wore on, Laura's father excused himself to check on the light once more before retiring, politely refusing the lieutenant's offer to do it for him. To Laura's surprise, Renten then offered to assist with cleaning the kitchen.

They chatted over the chores and she found out the lieutenant was from Dorset where his family still lived. He had a sister who was to have her coming-out next summer and a widowed mother who he was supporting.

Laura listened and waited for mention of a wife. The fact there was none made her unaccountably glad.

She told him about the offer to train under Miss Jones to become a school mistress in town and start as a teacher the following September, and of her interest in keeping meteorological records like her father.

Suddenly, as quick as a flash, Whisky raced across the kitchen again, under a chair, around a table leg, through Renten's legs and skidded on the slate floor to come to a halt right by the back door.

A strange note came from her throat, a chattering sound, not quite the same as her hunting sound.

"Whisky! What are you doing, you daft cat?" Laura called. "Shoo! Get away from the door, go sleep in front of the fire like your brother."

Over the wind outside, Laura could hear shuffling noises but dismissed them as nothing more than Milly and Acorn in their stalls.

The cat, its gaze fixed on the door, reversed a few paces, back arched and a ridge of fur rising up at the tail.

Laura reached for a broom propped in the corner when Renten grabbed it. Their hands barely touched but the warmth of his lingered as she allowed him to take it.

"I'm going outside to check."

Laura shook her head. "Really, there's no need, there's always odd sounds when the wind pushes on shore like this..."

He put a finger to his lips to silence her and unlatched the door, slipping around it and closing it behind him with nary a sound.

Laura continued tidying up and kicked herself.

He was being polite and you had to embarrass him and yourself.

Humph! 'Going outside to check'! How many times had her father used a similar excuse of 'going for a short stroll' to conveniently answer the call of nature?

Countless, countless times.

Laura Ann Rose Winter, you are a goose of the first order!

Yet that didn't explain why he took the broom...

Oh well. Least said, soonest mended, she thought.

The best thing would be to put Lieutenant Renten out of her mind. After all, the crossing to Ashton-On-Sea would soon be passable and him gone, chasing ne'er-do-wells, pirates and smugglers on behalf of the Crown.

Still, when she had thought of a man falling into her lap, she never considered he might be washed up on shore!

The thought made her giggle out loud and Admiral raised a sleepy head from his place at the fire to look at her.

Laura placed her hand over her mouth at the sound of boots at the kitchen door. It wouldn't do for him to see her like that.

The sound of the boots grew louder.

What on earth was he doing? Dancing a jig?

A figure burst through the door. She noticed a sharp blade glinting in the lamp light before realising the man was not Renten.

He grinned evilly and held the knife forward. Laura screamed.

Admiral leapt to his feet, fur standing on end making him near double in size. He ran straight in front of the advancing man, tripping and bringing him to his knees. His weapon clattered loose onto the floor

He swung a fist at Admiral and the cat yowled at the blow, then doubled back and with a one-two strike of his claws, drew blood from the back of the intruder's hand.

Laura picked up a small skillet and brought it down with a dull clang on the man's head. He gasped and slipped unconscious to the floor.

Another man burst through the doorway. Laura brandished her skillet and screamed again.

"It's me!" said Renten, raising his hands in a placating gesture. "I don't have time to explain. Lock all the doors and windows now. I'll deal with this one."

Startled by his sudden appearance, with thick dark hair wildly dishevelled by the wind and the alertness and command with which he carried himself, Laura hurried to comply.

"What's going on?" Laura's father yelled from the stairwell door, his face flushed with the exertion of rapidly descending the light house.

"The brigands are on the island," Renten called while he bound the still-unconscious invader hand and foot with strips of wash cloth.

From another part of the house there was the sound of breaking glass.

"Papa!" Laura called.

Renten arrived to her aid.

She stood to one side of her bedroom window armed with a fire poker, jabbing at the arm of the man trying to feel his way to the latch that would open the sash.

That wasn't working so she struck a forceful downward blow and the arm withdrew accompanied by a yowl of pain, along with a trail of blood.

Immediately another face appeared in the window. A bearded face, angry and scowling, that looked briefly into the room directly at the lieutenant then ducked away.

"Renten! Come out here, you scurvy dog! I thought your death was too good to be true. You've got more lives than a cat."

Laura turned to see Renten draw himself taller. It was clear he knew the man.

"I'm surprised the storm didn't put you in Davy Jones' locker," the lieutenant retorted.

"Not before I see you in hell with me!"

"Manners, Blackwell! There's a lady present!"

There was a momentary pause before the bearded face again loomed in the window, this time glancing left and right. Laura brandished her poker once more as the man's eyes fell upon her.

"Beggin' your pardon, miss," the scoundrel known as Blackwell said rather formally. "Now if you wouldn't mind persuading your houseguest to leave with us, then we will be all on our way peaceable like.

"You see, I have a dozen good strong men here who are capable of taking apart your cottage stone-by-stone."

Laura turned to look at Renten.

Then she saw her father appear at his shoulder and raise his musket.

Chapter Five

"I'll decide who is a guest in my home and who is not." Laura's father cocked the weapon to add emphasis. The click was crisp, unmistakable over the sound of the wind. The face in the window disappeared into the blackness outside.

"Well, it wouldn't do to be too hasty now, would it?" ventured Blackwell in a conciliating voice, a little distance away. "I'll tell you what I'll do. My men will keep guard while you all get a very nice night's sleep."

"I'll tell you what we'll do," Laura's father continued. "One of your men has already made himself at home here, so we'll keep him as our guest overnight."

"Which one, Renten?"

"Smithy," the lieutenant answered.

There was a grunt, then the sound of murmured voices as though a consensus was being sought.

"All right, keep the zounderkite for the night," agreed Blackwell. "We'll parley in the morning. First light."

Over the sound of the wind, the sound of tramping feet could be heard leaving the courtyard.

Renten swiftly opened the windows and pulled the storm shutters closed over the now broken windows. He turned back to his hosts and folded his arms. His expression was grim.

"Mr Winter, Miss Winter — you have my apologies," he said. "Should you wish to toss me out, I wouldn't blame you."

"Don't be daft, young man," Laura's father scoffed. "So what are we going to do to sort these blighters out?"

Laura watched Renten consider her and her father for several long seconds and she realised she was still gripping the poker. Her father held the musket across his chest.

Then a broad smile spread over his face. Laura felt her spirits lighten immediately.

"Well," said the lieutenant, "with Smithy safely tucked away, there are twelve of them and three of us. I think the odds are in our favour."

He turned to Laura. "Miss Winter... Laura," he continued, "I suggest you get some sleep. It's going to be a long night."

Laura was prepared to argue when her father stepped in.

"The clockwork will need to be wound twice more before morning, dear girl, and I'll need to show the lieutenant the caves."

Renten looked intrigued. "Caves? Are they easy to find?"

Laura's father shook his head slowly and grinned. "They're not and no one knows the Rock better than me."

"It looks like I'm outnumbered, but you—" she said to Renten, poking his chest with a finger, "you make sure my father doesn't lead you into trouble."

He gifted her with a wink.

"I'm good at following orders... more or less."

As the beam of light swept around, Laura could see a schooner at anchor off the island. A small bonfire burned on the headland, highlighting four small tents. Earlier, she saw figures walking about but Blackwell was apparently being as good as his word.

As the night wore on and Laura wound the clockwork mechanism for the last time before dawn, the fire on the headland had burned down to glowing red coals.

She must have slept after that, with Whisky and Admiral curled up beside her, because she wasn't awakened by the pre dawn light but by an insistent knock on the door below.

"Miss Laura!" She recognised the lieutenant's voice. "Quick as you can. Join us downstairs."

Had she missed something? She straightened herself quickly and swiftly descended the spiral staircase. Her father was in the kitchen; the smell of cured ham and eggs along with the earthy pungent aroma of freshly fried mushrooms filled the room.

He handed his daughter a full plate — a man-sized serving. She was about to protest when he pivoted across on his good leg to grasp the back of a chair at the table where Renten sat tucking into his food.

He sat down, taking several mouthfuls of food before he noticed his daughter standing there looking at him askance.

"Eat up, dear girl, we have a lot of work to do."

Laura slowly sank into her chair and put a forkful of food into her mouth. Her father looked ten years younger. She hadn't seen that spark in his eyes since her mother passed away.

"What do you two have planned?" she asked, suspicion dripping from each word.

Renten put a finger up to ask for silence as he shovelled the last of his breakfast into his mouth and washed it down with a swig of tea.

"Your father showed me through the caves."

Ah, thought Laura, that explains the mushrooms for breakfast.

"All I need is some blue powder, black powder and a little time."

Renten and her father's enthusiasm was infectious and Laura found herself catching it too.

"What do you need me to do?"

A fourth had joined them after breakfast, albeit reluctantly. Smithy was seated miserably at the table, his bound hands and feet covered by a large cloak, his dirty pale hair plastered with a mixture of coal dust and fat to darken it.

At a distance he would pass for the lieutenant. A musket aimed at his head by Laura's father ensured his ongoing compliance.

Laura waited at the back door until she heard the cellar door close. Renten was on his way through the narrow and dark labyrinth of caves and fissures that would open out to the sea.

Her father remained out of sight and nodded.

She emerged into the morning sun and the courtyard seemed deserted, although she was certain someone would be watching, hence the ruse with Smithy.

Adjusting the empty basket on her arm, Laura turned to see a man emerge from the shadows.

He had an overnight growth of whiskers only, so he was not Blackwell.

"'Owdie miss," he greeted with a laconic drawl as he made his way towards her.

"Good morning," she said crisply.

"'Ow's our friend inside then?"

"Look for yourself."

The man did and saw a black-haired figure sitting with his back to the window.

"Excuse me," said Laura, sweeping past him. "I have eggs to collect."

Laura opened the door to the coop and the chickens rushed out, following their long-practised routine of milling in the courtyard before rushing out the gate and onto the grass.

Inside the coop, Laura reached into the laying box to collect the eggs, mindful of the man watching her. Then she felt her bottom being pinched.

Laura stood, banged her head on a roost and let out a yelp of surprise.

There followed immediately another high-pitched scream but it didn't come from her. Wild flapping filled the air and Laura stood back as the man tried frantically to protect his face from the wild pecking and scratching of the coop's very angry rooster, King.

He stumbled backwards out into the courtyard and ran blindly in a small circle with the rooster attached to his head. "Help! Help!" he cried, but when he dislodged the fowl after several frenzied seconds, it was too late to stop from crashing headlong into the courtyard wall.

The man slumped to the ground and King shook himself down and strutted outside to join the hens.

Laura slipped out of the coop and bolted the door behind her, regarding the unconscious man with satisfaction. One down, eleven to go. She calmly released Milly from her pen and Acorn from his stall before returning to the house.

"Father?" she called, bolting the door.

"In here, my girl."

She found him in the parlour where it appeared Smithy was now being made 'comfortable' in front of the bay window. Then the figure slumped forward.

"What happened to him?"

Laura's father hauled the figure back up but it was not Smithy. The cloak was now wrapped about her father's bolster pillow with collar turned up and a broad-brimmed hat covering the 'head'. It seemed that her father had fashioned a mannequin.

"I couldn't leave Smithy to help you so I tossed him back in the cupboard," he said by way of explanation.

"Then I saw you and King had sorted the other one out so I threw this together."

Laura nodded at the mannequin. "That's not going to fool Blackwell for long."

"It doesn't have to — just for long enough."

"Well, you're going to get your chance," said Laura, pointing out of the window. "Here comes Blackwell now."

They watched the menacing figure approach the front door with purpose.

Then a series of crackles and pops disturbed the morning air as a bright white flare burst in the sky past the window, and sea birds screeched and flew away from the noise.

Laura and her father rushed outside.

Beneath the flare burst, at a distance, Renten stood with his back to the cliff on the shoreside of the Rock. At his feet sat a small iron cauldron and a candle stub in a glass lantern.

"There he is, grab him!" yelled Blackwell to two of his men. The pair sprinted across the grass with Blackwell following.

Laura's father put a restraining hand on her arm, bringing her to a stop just outside the door.

"There's nothing we can do from here."

"But—"

"Just wait."

The two men had now pulled out their swords and yelled damnable threats as they closed in.

"What doesn't the lieutenant do something?" Laura whispered tautly.

"Just wait," her father insisted.

Blackwell too had stopped running as he watched his two men close the gap. They were now only ten yards away when Renten picked up the lantern, pulled out the candle and dropped it in the cauldron.

The blackguards closed in — five yards, two yards — then the powder in the cauldron ignited. Renten disappeared in a flash of light and billowing smoke.

The two men ran into the miasma and, a moment later, their cries of distress were heard as they ran right off the edge of the cliff.

Laura gripped her father's hand at the sound and the sight. When the white-blue smoke cleared and the cliff edge was deserted, save for the cauldron.

Chapter Six

Laura cried out but her father held her firm. She looked at him but he kept his head down in case Blackwell, standing aghast only a hundred feet away, turned and saw him grinning.

"Calm yourself, dear girl," her father reassured her as Blackwell now ran over to the cliff edge, "not everything is as it appears. Trust me — the lieutenant is perfectly safe."

More of Blackwell's men joined him on the cliff edge and he ordered them to descend in search of their companions.

Laura cocked her head. "What have you and he been up to?"

"No time to talk now. Get up the tower, my girl, and hoist a new message. We need help from the shore."

Laura nodded, already mentally counting out the signal flags she would need.

"What are you going to be doing?" she asked.

"I'll secure the cottage then join you in the lighthouse. Shortly, our friend Mister Blackwell will not be happy."

Satisfied with the arrangements, Laura retrieved the flag box and climbed halfway up the stairs to the small tower window. She pulled the previous signal in like so much laundry, and set the new message.

She completed the climb to the top and looked out. Even without a spyglass, Laura could see stirring on the shore already. She chanced a look over in the other direction. A flushed and angry Blackwell stood halfway between the cliff-edge and the lighthouse, looking up at the signal flags and her. Laura offered a cheeky wave.

His face turned a furious puce shade before he turned and erupted into a tremendous bellow to his men on the edge of the cliff now hauling their injured compatriots up off the rocks below.

Milly the goat wandered into view, her ears erect at Blackwell's roar. Laura watched the animal's head drop as it ran as fast as her four little legs could take her — right at Blackwell's rear.

The man was cannoned onto his face and Milly bleated her satisfaction before trotting off.

Laura doubled over in laughter but then stopped abruptly as a door slammed downstairs and there came the sound of drawers being opened and closed violently. Her heart pounded. The villains were inside and ransacking her home!

Then came her father's voice: "Laura! Where's my telescope?"

Her heart resumed its normal rhythm.

"I have it up here with me," she called down.

She heard him close and bolt the connecting door to the tower and start making his way, seat first, up the stairs.

"Head up to the light and tell me what you see," he called ahead.

From her advantage point, she could see Blackwell had regathered what remained of his dignity and his men. The leader gesticulated wildly with his brandished cutlass. She then trained the telescope across to Ashton-On-Sea.

The townsfolk, attracted by the flare, were now reacting to the flags. She saw Mr Fletcher and Dickie, the Reverend Harman and a few other townsmen casting off in the roiling and choppy waves that still separated St Joseph's Rock from the shore.

Laura relayed the information to her father.

"And what of Renten?" his disembodied voice demanded. "Check the schooner!"

"The schooner? How on earth did he get there?"

She edged around the lantern to look south though the telescope. Renten was just bringing a dinghy alongside the boat.

Her father spoke from the doorway as he struggled to his feet.

"Where the lieutenant dropped off the edge of the cliff is a small ledge and fissure. You know the Rock is full of them. That one leads across to the ocean side but is narrow and hazardous. The lieutenant's mission was to draw Blackwell's men shore side then slip through to their vessel."

Laura put the glass back to her eye and could see the lieutenant's dark hair ruffle in the breeze and his shirt stretched taut across his back as he hefted a small barrel on to his shoulder.

"What in heaven's name is he doing?"

Renten nimbly climbed up a rope ladder and tossed the barrel on the deck before scrambling up over the deck rail himself.

"He has a surprise planned for our visitors," said her father, limping to her side.

Laura passed the telescope to him. To her surprise, he didn't spare a moment looking at Renten, but instead set the focus on the brigands on the ground.

They too had noticed the two small boats from Ashton-On-Sea making their way to Saint Joseph's Rock. Blackwell's men had gathered around him.

Without the advantage of the telescope, Laura could only guess at what they were saying. They did not look at all pleased.

"We need more time," he father muttered, handing her the telescope once again.

"More time for what?" she asked to an empty room. Her father was already making his way downstairs.

She followed after him.

"Father!"

He was hobbling precariously down the stairs for speed, putting the least weight possible on his injured foot.

"We need a further distraction. The signal cannon should do it," he called back to her.

Laura followed him into the kitchen where he opened the pantry door. From behind a sack of potatoes, he pulled out a small barrel similar to the one she had seen the lieutenant carrying.

"Gunpowder! Mother would be cross with you bringing a whole barrel into the house!"

He ignored her scolding, instead telling her to fetch along a couple of the small cannon balls he had hidden among the onions.

Outside, on the eastern side of the lighthouse, the small cannon stood pointing out to sea.

Her father prepared the cannon, priming it with gunpowder and lighting the fuse as Laura nervously waited for them to be discovered by one of Blackwell's men.

As good fortune would have it, they remained out of sight behind the cottage, arguing volubly with their leader.

"Right-o Laura, get back inside—"

Bang!

The little cannon fired, the report disproportionately loud to its small size, and it immediately attracted attention.

In fact, before they could go more than a few paces, ten men with cutlasses drawn stood between them and the safety of the cottage.

Blackwell stepped forward.

"You," he thundered, his arm shaking with fury as he pointed to them. "You two have become too meddlesome."

"Big Arms! No Nose! Take them inside and tie them up." The two men who stepped forward clearly deserved their nicknames. The two men pinned their arms behind their backs and began marching them towards the cottage, Laura's father moaning in pain at being forced to put weight on his injured ankle.

Behind them, Blackwell roared at his men.

"The rest of you find that fool Smithy and look for Tinder while you're at it. He's not been seen since first light. He can't have gone far on this flyspeck."

Close to the cottage, the lighthouse keeper stumbled.

"Father!" Laura cried out in alarm. "You big brute, let go of me. My father is hurt!"

After a few strong tugs, No Nose decided to let her go. She rushed to her father and wrapped her arms around him.

"Just a few moments more," he muttered. "A few moments more..."

"Hey! What you be mutterin' 'bout?" Big Arms asked.

Laura helped her father back to his feet and he took a hesitant step towards the cottage. Then a smile split his face as a flash of light, brighter than the sun, reflected in the cottage windows.

Laura turned rapidly to see the strange phenomenon and a fraction later the sound caught up.

BOOM!

O ne of the schooner's large spars shot a hundred feet straight up in the air, and Laura watched agog as the large lump of timber began falling.

"Thunderation!" exclaimed Big Arms. He and No Nose took off in the direction of the blast though it was clear they could do little about it.

Laura's father tugged her towards shelter as debris began raining down on the Rock.

Acorn galloped as fast as Laura had ever seen him, quickly followed by Milly and the chickens which all huddled in the courtyard vocalising their distress, the sound echoing around the stone enclosure.

Admiral and Whisky peered out from behind a curtain, their tawny eyes wide and round.

Blackwell and his men stood at the southerly point where their schooner was now nothing more than flotsam.

"Quick as you can, love, back inside," Laura's father urged. "If Blackwell was angry before, he's going to be furious now."

"What are you going to do?"

"I'm going to meet our friends from Ashton."

Laura shook off her father's hand and ran back to where No Nose and Big Arms had dropped their weapons as they fled. She picked up both blades and returned with them.

"*We're* going to meet our friends from Ashton," she corrected him. "No one is going to drive me out of my home."

She thought her father may be angry at her disobedience. Instead he grinned and urged her to run ahead of him.

"That's my girl," he muttered with pride.

By the time they had reached the path that rose from the submerged causeway, Reverend Harman, Fletcher and Dickie had been joined by a group of twenty other men — fishermen and farmhands, smithies and merchants — all of them angry.

"Where are the scurvy-dog scoundrels!" demanded one.

"We'll drive them back into the sea!" added another.

Reverend Harman called for calm and Laura's father told the story of the past three nights.

The crowd grumbled.

"Eh Dickie, you bring enough rope to secure these blackguards?" asked Fletcher of his assistant.

The young man pushed his way forward with a coil of rope across his shoulder.

"I did, sir!" he said, bustling to the fore.

The grocer leaned in. "Now that would be the old stock, not the new that came in the other day?" he muttered.

"Oh, yes, Mr Fletcher, the old stuff just like you said."

"Good lad," replied the older man, then, noticing the reproachful looks from the others, he straightened his back and rubbed his belly. "It's still good rope, well proven..."

"Then round them up, men," Reverend Harman instructed, rolling up his sleeves, apparently ready to put his boxing skills to the test if need be. "These villains can cool their heels in one of the empty warehouses until the Waterguard arrives in the morning."

With the exception of the Reverend, Laura noted, everyone was armed — cutlasses, pistols, hoes and clubs — and they marched with purpose towards the southern point where Blackwell and his men remained, disconsolate at their loss.

At the sound of the approaching posse, Blackwell turned. A menacing grin spread slowly across his face. He may have lost his ship but it seemed he still enjoyed a fight.

He drew his cutlass and stepped forward.

"We're not going to surrender meekly to a group of lily-livered townsfolks, are we men?" he called.

"Yes we are!" they replied.

Blackwell turned back glacially.

"Men?"

They looked at one another. Big Arms, who appeared to have been appointed spokesman of those who remained fit for battle, stepped forward, rubbing the back of his head ruefully.

"Actually, Mr Blackwell, the men 'ave all agreed we're going to give up smuggling."

Murmured agreement rippled through the gang.

"I mean, it's one thing to bring in contraband from the Frenchies, but tying up that customs man and throwing him overboard in a storm was criminal."

"You *are* criminals!" Blackwell insisted.

"Aye, but we're not murderers."

One by one the men dropped their weapons and raised their arms above their heads — all except Blackwell who was quickly disarmed and restrained by two of the blacksmith's men.

"Sir, miss," said Big Arms, addressing Laura and her father. "I'm very sorry to have 'arrassed you. You won't have any trouble from us again, I'll promise ye that."

Laura's father nodded his acknowledgement but she had lost interest in the proceedings.

She wandered to the edge of the cliff. The sea was beginning to calm, already returning to the rhythm of the days and the seasons which were long familiar to her.

It tugged at her, filling her with a strange longing.

The sun had moved past its zenith and golden tipped waves shimmered on the horizon. Amid the debris from the schooner, the small boat from the vessel was bobbing near the rocks, unattended.

The lieutenant!

She hadn't seen him since the explosion. Was he safe? Had he fallen overboard? Had he made it off the boat at all?

His absence jolted her into action.

At the northern end of the Rock, the prisoners were already being ferried across to the mainland in groups.

Now there was only a handful of men waiting for transport. Her father was speaking to the Reverend.

"Father, have you seen Lieutenant Renten?" she interrupted.

"There he is," he said, pointing to one of the boats making its way back to Ashton-On-Sea with the prisoners. Laura's heart skipped a beat as she identified him from his dark hair.

As though he was aware of being observed, he turned and appeared to be looking straight at her.

No, surely that couldn't be; he was four hundred yards away and yet he raised his hand and gave a salute. She raised her hand in return and his salute turned into a wave.

Despite the chill in the air, warmth bloomed through her.

What remained of the month of December raced through like the squalls that sweep in from the Atlantic.

The excitement caused by the arrival of the brigands ebbed after as Blackwell and his men were taken away. Life returned to normal.

The fleet went out to catch fish between the winter storms and this year's Ashton-On-Sea Christmas fete was judged to be the best yet.

With his foot fully healed, Laura's father had taken his place in the choir, much to the delight of Miss Jones who also invited Laura to teach the youngest children at her school after New Year instead of waiting until the next school year.

Yet despite the festivities and parties, Laura felt something amiss.

Lieutenant Michael Renten.

How odd that someone she had only known for a short time and under the most extraordinary circumstances should occupy so much of her thoughts.

She had been among the townsfolk gathered on the quay to farewell the dashing young officer but in the press of the crowd it would be a mistake to believe that, as he stood looking back on the gangplank, he was looking for her.

And surely it was a silly romantic notion, born of reading too many novels, that it seemed to her their eyes met for that briefest moment before he was urged on to the clipper by the bosun.

Laura never spoke these thoughts aloud.

Only a private diary knew her secrets — a record of one moment in time when she had a brush with adventure and romance — a precious memory to treasure.

Perhaps that would be enough.

Chapter Eight

Christmas Day

St Joseph's Church on Ashton-on-Sea was beautifully lit that morning. A myriad of candles burned in every candelabra, casting a merry yellow light on the colourful hand sewn silk pennants that hung from the walls.

Laura wore her warmest wool dress in a deep red. It was a festive colour which matched her mood. On her coat was a lovely gold-enamelled brooch, a gift from her father.

Reverend Harman delivered the sermon from the Book of Isaiah:

> For unto us a Child is born,
> Unto us a Son is given;
> And the government will be upon His shoulder.
> And His name will be called
> Wonderful, Counsellor, Mighty God

The choir took up the theme with excerpts from Handel's Messiah which they had been rehearsing since September.

Laura listened proudly to her father's rich tenor. He looked wonderful in his choir robes of scarlet red and white.

As the recital continued, Laura felt a small rush of cold air brush across her shoulder as latecomers joined them.

Not very surprising, she thought, not glancing back but enraptured by the candle-lit choir. Summer might bring the sun worshippers looking to take a rest cure by the sea, but Christmas brought the pilgrims looking to capture a moment of spiritual connection, no matter how tenuously arrived.

The choir did not disappoint with its recital, nor Reverend Harman when he stepped forward and read Blake's poem, the one adopted for St Joseph's Rock.

> *And did those feet in ancient time*
> *Walk upon England's mountains green?*
> *And was the holy Lamb of God*
> *On England's pleasant pastures seen?*

As the congregation stood together to sing Hark! The Herald Angels Sing, Laura could not help but think of Blackwell's brigands during the opening verse and she wished them reconciled too.

Outside after the service, she looked across to the lighthouse, its tall whitewashed tower gleaming in the winter sun. The tides favoured them today. It would be hours before they needed to consider a homeward journey.

Laura spotted a familiar face and rushed towards him.

"Dickie! Congratulations, I'm so glad you proposed." Laura hugged Dickie, then Kitty, a pretty little blonde girl, the daughter of the local tailor who was receiving well wishes from everyone in the parish.

Even Mr Fletcher who was normally so gruff with his assistant stood beaming with avuncular pride.

"Tell me, Laura," said Kitty, "who is your father talking to?"

"I'm not sure," she admitted. The man must have been among their latecomers but he had his back to her.

He was dressed in the uniform of a naval Commander — crisp white breeches topped by a rich navy blue coat trimmed with gold braiding and buttons on the sleeves. A single gold epaulette sat on the left shoulder.

Then, for the first time, she noticed the other smartly dressed naval officers among the congregation. She looked for a lieutenant's uniform and found it. Its wearer was talking to the reverend's wife.

Laura turned away.

It wasn't him.

"Laura!"

Disappointment dampened her cheer but she forced a smile and turned to her father's call.

"There is someone who is very keen to renew acquaintances."

The commander turned and she found herself face to face with the man who filled her dreams and the pages of her diary.

"Miss Winter, a great pleasure to see you again."

His warm and ready smile faltered for a moment before Laura realised she hadn't returned his greeting but was simply staring at him open-mouthed.

She recovered herself.

"The pleasure is mine, *Commander*."

To her surprise, he blushed and his smile turned shy.

"My commission is only a week old. I'm still not used to hearing it," he admitted.

"With your father's permission, would you care to take a walk, Miss Winter?"

To Laura's mind, her father gave his permission with too much enthusiasm, even excusing himself before she could accept the offer herself.

Renten offered his arm and she took it and they strolled toward the Strand.

The quayside no longer bore evidence of the storm but was now home to three new ships she didn't recognise — a fine single-masted cutter, an elegant sloop and a smaller boat better suited for navigating the shallow inlets along the coast.

"We arrived just as the service was beginning. I came straight to the church," he said.

He told her that after Blackwell's capture, due in no short measure to her and her father, he was promoted.

"I asked to take a brand new posting, right here," he said.

"How long has my father known?"

"A week, possibly two. I wrote to ask permission to court you when I learned of my promotion. Why?"

He paused and grinned as the answer came to him.

"He never told you did he?"

"He did not! The sneak."

"Disappointed?"

"Never," she said sincerely.

Laura stepped closer. She could feel his warmth and she placed both hands in his and squeezed them gently.

He raised her hand to his lips and kissed it.

"In fact," she said, "It is a Christmas wish come true."

Then let us all rejoice again,
On Christmas Day, on Christmas Day;
Then let us all rejoice again,
On Christmas Day in the morning

THE END

ABOUT THE AUTHOR

Elizabeth Ellen Carter has won praise and a wide readership for her highly researched historical romance adventures.

The novella *The Thief of Hearts* was first published in 2016 for Christmas.

The short story *Three Ships* was written for the free eBook anthology *A Season To Remember: Four Short Stories For Christmas* and first published in 2014

For more information, visit eecarter.com and subscribe to her magazine Love's Great Adventure at eecarter.com/book-club

TITLES BY
ELIZABETH ELLEN CARTER

Moonstone Obsession

Moonstone Conspiracy

Warrior's Surrender

Dark Heart

Captive of the Corsairs

Revenge of the Corsairs

Shadow of the Corsairs

Nocturne

The Thief of Hearts

COMING IN 2018-2019

The King's Rogues (Four Book Series)

LEARN MORE AT EECARTER.COM
OR SEARCH
'ELIZABETH ELLEN CARTER'
ON AMAZON

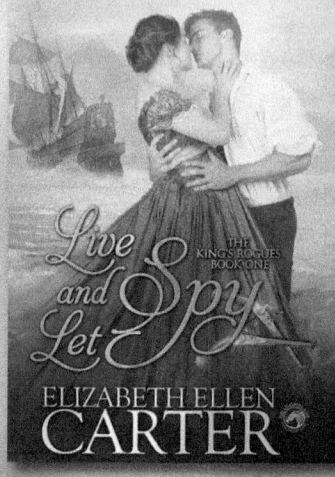

Live and Let Spy
THE KING'S ROGUES
BOOK ONE
ELIZABETH ELLEN
CARTER

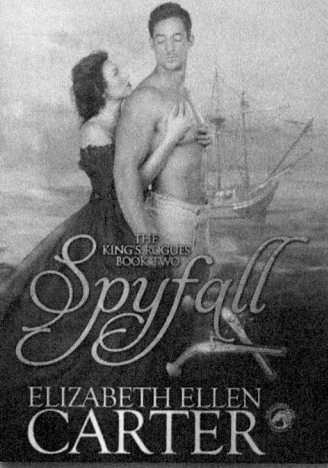

THE KING'S ROGUES
BOOK TWO
Spyfall
ELIZABETH ELLEN
CARTER

COMING 2018-2019

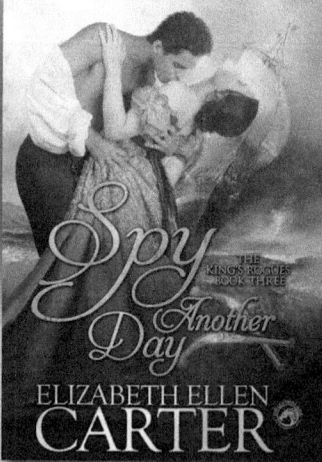

Spy
THE KING'S ROGUES
BOOK THREE
Another Day
ELIZABETH ELLEN
CARTER

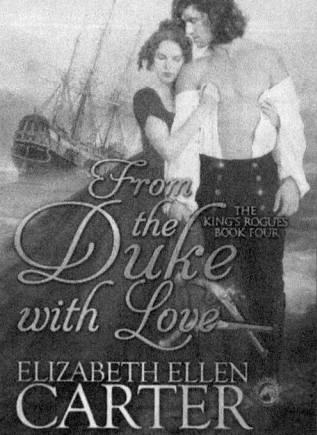

From the Duke with Love
THE KING'S ROGUES
BOOK FOUR
ELIZABETH ELLEN
CARTER

COMING FROM
ELIZABETH ELLEN CARTER

ADAM HARDACRE SHOULD BE AN OFFICER IN HIS MAJESTY'S ROYAL NAVY BUT HIS LOW BIRTH CONDEMNS HIM TO THE NON-COMMISSIONED RANKS. HOWEVER, WHEN HE TRIES TO QUIT, HE'S MADE AN OFFER TOO TEMPTING TO REFUSE - CREATE A BAND OF ADVENTURERS WHO WILL SPY IN THE SERVICE OF ENGLAND AGAINST NAPOLEON.

ALL UNOFFICIALLY, OF COURSE...

THEY'RE NOT AGENTS OF THE CROWN - THEY'RE THE KING'S ROGUES.

Adam recalled his terrified sixteen-year-old self—young with no experience, but a world of opportunity ahead of him. Now he was a man with experience, but no opportunity. Well, he couldn't sit like a lumpen on this park bench until the end of time. He got to his feet.

"I hope you're not leaving on my account."

He swiftly turned. It was the civilian from the Admiralty. "No, by all means," said Adam. "Take the bench, take the park... take the devil too, for all I care. I'm leaving."

The stranger grinned, clearly amused. "I wanted to see you before I left London," he said. "And I'm much obliged to you for making it easy. I thought it would take days to find the tavern you were drowning your sorrows in."

"Who the hell do you think you are?"

The man reached into his dark blue coat and withdrew a thick white card. "I am Lord Daniel Ridgeway, and I have a proposition for you. Come to Charteris House three weeks from now." Before Adam could draw breath to refuse, Ridgeway reached back into his coat pocket and pulled out a thickish envelope. "Fifty pounds. Consider it a signing bounty."

Adam regarded the envelope. "I could walk away now and be fifty pounds the richer with no obligation to you."

"You could. But you won't."

"You seem very sure of yourself."

Ridgeway grinned again. "I know what sort of man I'm dealing with."

- from Book 1, Live And Let Spy
Coming in 2018 from Dragonblade Publishing